"Dante, there is nothing I want to do more right now than this."

And Lucie held his eyes, then leaned forward to cup his face. Still Dante held back. Until her tongue eased his lips apart and slid into his mouth.

"Please don't stop," she breathed, tightening her legs and tilting her hips. She reached her arms up and pulled him down into a kiss he could no more resist than his next breath. She defined *irresistible*.

Her eyes, when she opened them to see why he had stopped, were anxious.

"Lucie, are you sure you've done this before?" he asked, not even knowing himself that those words were going to come out of his mouth. It seemed ridiculous—but he had to know...

She glanced away.

"Sweetheart?"

"I never said I had or I hadn't, but I want to—so badly. Please, Dante."

"Are you telling me you're a *virgin*?" He shook his head at his own stupidity. She was so adamant. So resolute. And she just *did* it for him. Completely.

When she didn't answer, he rolled that around for a bewildered second even as she moved under him, used the legs hooked round his back to pull him nearer.

"Oh, angel, you're killing me."

Claimed by a Billionaire

*Commanding and charismatic, these men
take what—and who—they want!*

Dante Hermida, polo player and playboy
extraordinaire, meets the only woman
to tame him in

The Argentinian's Virgin Conquest

April 2017

Billionaire tycoon Marco Borsatto has never
forgiven Stacey Jackson's betrayal, but he's
never forgotten their chemistry... Meeting
her again, he's determined that this time,
she will never forget him!

The Italian's Vengeful Seduction

May 2017

You won't want to miss this dramatically intense,
scorchingly sexy duet from Bella Frances!

Bella Frances

—

THE ARGENTINIAN'S VIRGIN CONQUEST

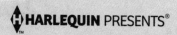

Recycling programs
for this product may
not exist in your area.

ISBN-13: 978-0-373-06060-3

The Argentinian's Virgin Conquest

First North American Publication 2017

Copyright © 2017 by Bella Frances

HARLEQUIN®
www.Harlequin.com

Printed in U.S.A.

Unable to sit still without reading, **Bella Frances** first found romantic fiction at the age of twelve, in between deadly dull knitting patterns and recipes in the pages of her grandmother's magazines. An obsession was born! But it wasn't until one long, hot summer, after completing her first degree in English literature, that she fell upon the legends that are Harlequin books. She has occasionally lifted her head out of them since to do a range of jobs, including barmaid, financial adviser and teacher, as well as to practice (but never perfect) the art of motherhood to two (almost grown-up) cherubs.

Bella lives a very energetic life in the UK but tries desperately to travel for pleasure at least once a month—strictly in the interests of research!

Catch up with her on her website at bellafrances.co.uk.

Books by Bella Frances

Harlequin Presents

The Playboy of Argentina
The Scandal Behind the Wedding

Harlequin KISS

Dressed to Thrill

Visit the Author Profile page at Harlequin.com for more titles.

To my daughter Katie, filling the world with love, everywhere she goes. I couldn't be more proud. X

CHAPTER ONE

IT WAS ONE thing to plan the perfect party—it was another thing entirely to pull it off. The Honourable Lucinda Bond of Strathdee knew that better than anyone. Oh, yes. Sipping a scalding mouthful of a really rather bitter Americano, she made yet another mental note of how she would improve things next time.

Next time! As if there would ever be a next time...

Down in the galley kitchen of her infamous father's infamous yacht she could hear voices rise and explode between the chef and the caterers.

Lucinda—Lucie to her very few friends—stepped out onto the nearest sleekly polished deck to get a moment to herself, but there was no escape. The fierce Caribbean sun was already causing the air to throb, and the flotilla of little boats and giant yachts that were moored off Petit Pierre reminded her more of a flock of killer seagulls than a flutter of happy butterflies.

Honestly. What on earth had possessed her to have

this charity auction, the biggest bash of the season, in aid of her beloved Caribbean Conservation Centre, here in the Bahamas, on the *Marengo*, with a guest list to die for and a crippling lack of confidence as deep as the Caribbean Sea?

Money. Dollars—Bahamian or American. Pounds. Euros. It didn't really matter at the end of the day. As long as her sanctuary—her pride, her joy, her reason for being in this hot, bright heaven— got every last cent from the people who would soon be treading all over her father's floating emporium.

Her stomach lurched again, but the calm, flat sea definitely wasn't to blame. The thought of this party tonight was.

As long as *she* came—Lady Viv, her mother.

As long as she came to call the auction and schmooze the crowd everything would be fine. No one would give a damn about Lucie and her crippling social anxiety if her glamorous, glorious mother dropped from the sky in her helicopter and beamed her brilliant smile all around. She was adored by public and press alike. Loved for her golden hair, her sparkling eyes and her utterly perfect figure.

The fact that she had an utterly imperfect style of parenting was neither here nor there. The world had no idea that the custody battle that had raged between her mother and father had been more about each having *less* time with her than more. All they knew was that she'd had enough of her husband's affairs and had decided to have one herself—with

James Haston-Black, or 'Badass Black', as he was known. Glamorous divorcees sold many more newspapers than neglected children, after all.

Lucie swilled the final inch of bitter dark liquid around the cup, then tossed it back. She screwed up her face and shuddered, wishing desperately that she could drink full-fat lattes instead of these vile brews. Soon. As soon as tonight was over she would unhook the unforgiving satin frock, screw it in a ball and head to the fridge without a care in the world. She would eat what she wanted and drink what she wanted. She would slob about in shorts and T-shirts and wash her hair when she felt like it. She would exercise by lifting food to her mouth. She would pack her make-up bag away in a drawer and smash her bathroom scales with a sledgehammer. End of.

Well, she might...

Her mother's 'conditions' for flying halfway across the world to host this party were fierce, but she had met them. Three months of abject misery—lose ten pounds, drop two dress sizes, style her hair, tone those 'thunder thighs'. Each and every obstacle—or 'betterment', as her mother described them—she had overcome. But this was the end. In ten hours' time she would be wearing the dress and smiling at the rich and the beautiful and counting all those lovely pennies.

And five hours after that she would be counting her blessings. If she pulled this off without having a panic attack or throwing herself overboard then a miracle would indeed have happened.

Lucie looked up at the place she had felt most happy in her whole life. The verdant green island, with its dormant volcano and swathe of blue ocean, truly was one of the prettiest islands in the Bahamas. And the fact that she had spent so much of her childhood there, especially in the years after her mother had left, made it doubly important. No one here cared that she was minor aristocracy, with a father who was more interested in dogs and horses than anything that had two legs—unless the legs belonged to a pretty young woman. No one here really cared about her mother either. Each second of life was just too succulent for them to bother about what Lady Vivienne Bond—as she would be known for ever, despite the divorce—was wearing to someone's party on the other side of the Atlantic.

Life here, in every stolen moment, was simple, happy, and as beautiful as the calypso music played all over the island. Lucie wasn't 'hiding', as Lady Viv claimed. *She* simply didn't understand that anyone could find pleasure working with smelly animals in a conservation centre, whereas Lucie couldn't understand how anyone could find pleasure wading through all those air-kisses at parties.

Much like what was going to happen tonight.

Yeuch.

She looked back over her shoulder at the ballroom—one of the many rooms on this three-hundred-foot yacht that would be used for the auction tonight, and was already being decorated by a silent swarm of staff who were transforming the darkly elegant interiors into something from a thirties musical film set.

She had taken care of promotion and ticket sales, passing on the growing list of familiar and unfamiliar names to her mother, Some of them had caused a seismic shift when she'd heard them.

'Urgh! Dante Hermida! He's a polo player and an utter Lothario. You'd best stay well away—though, having said that, you're probably not his type. Really, darling, you should put more effort into knowing who's who,' she'd added, when Lucie had reeled from yet another spray of her mother's vitriol.

A lull in the rapid exchanges from the galley allowed her to hear that her phone was ringing. Lucie looked at where it lay, face down on top of a pile of crisp napkins. It couldn't be Lady Viv—she was supposed to be halfway across the Atlantic by now. But even as she took the four paces across the deck she knew just whose image would be flashing.

God, no. She couldn't… Not this time…

Sure enough, her mother's iridescent smile flashed up at her. Lucie lifted the phone and stabbed the green call symbol like a crazy person.

'Why are you phoning? Where *are* you? Why aren't you on your way?'

She waited, clearly imagining the slight roll of her mother's artfully lined eyes and the slight twitch of her perfectly painted lips.

'Darling, *must* you answer your telephone in such a belligerent manner?'

Lucie clenched her eyes closed and prayed for composure.

'We'll overlook it for now and begin again. Good morning, Lucinda. I trust you slept well?'

Lucie was in no mood to play her games.

'Where are you, Mother?'

There was a slight pause—long enough for her to know that she was right. Her gut had told her that she would be left high and dry with this, that her mother would let her down yet again, but she had refused to believe it—refused to believe she could be so cruel. She *knew* just how much Lucie hated social situations, but one in which *she* would have to host was inconceivable.

Her mother was babbling on in her ear, but what did it matter? It was just one more example of where she featured in her mother's list—Badass Black at the top, then her beautiful boy Simon, then her friends, her charities, her houses, clothes and jewellery—and the thing lolling about at the bottom was Lucie.

'I'm calling to say I might be a little late.'

She sounded clipped, defensive. Or was that just wishful thinking?

'I'm almost sure I will still manage to make it—some of it—but things are really rather difficult at the moment... I'm sure Simon has got himself into a little trouble, and I can't just up and off until I know he's all right!'

Simon and trouble were like strawberries and cream. For twenty years her half-brother had been getting himself into trouble. He was quite the expert.

'I know your little party is important to you, but clearly I have to look after Simon—and, really, it was a bit selfish to expect that I could drop everything and fly over the Atlantic for something as trivial as a *tortoise*, or whatever it is, when I've got all these other commitments...'

Lucie didn't hear the end of the sentence. She stood in a daze, hearing the crystal clipped vowels and imagining the perfect nails drumming. James Haston-Black would be pouring a Scotch and Simon Haston-Black would be lying in someone's bed, lining up his next party.

And Lucie? She would be getting on with it. Herself.

She wondered if she would ever, *ever* feature to her mother as anything other than the irritating, overweight, unattractive daughter of her first husband.

'I have to go,' she said woodenly into the air, and then stood. Her shoulders sank and her head dipped and a sigh as heavy and wide as the gunmetal skies of home poured from her soul.

'Go where?' her mother whined, her voice like claws on thin wood. 'Look, Lucie, you'll be absolutely fine. You've watched me a thousand times. You simply speak into the microphone, pick a face in the crowd. And *smile*!'

'I have to get some—air. I have to go. For a swim.'

Lucie's mouth almost formed her *Love to Simon, love to James* standard response, but this time it choked her. She swallowed it back.

'Love you, Mother,' she said, and she clicked off the call, powered off the phone and walked, one flat sole after another, to her cabin. She'd clear her head. She'd work this out. She had to. Because, once again, she had no other option.

It was the morning after the night before—and the night before that—and if he could focus enough he knew that he might be able to recall exactly when this party had started. Because for Dante Salvatore Vidal Hermida—Dante to his several thousand friends, acquaintances and fans—this was turning into one hell of a hangover. Not that he had been drinking too much—he'd long since outgrown *that* particular route to oblivion. But the whole effort involved in happily hosting was catching up with him.

What he needed now was a clear run of mindless athleticism before getting back on a horse and leading the team to the glory of the Middle Eastern circuit.

There were noises behind him—a slurred squeal, a crash, a muffled laugh—and there was only so much more he could stomach. It was already nearly eleven a.m., and the day surely held a lot more than getting back 'on it' with Vasquez and Raoul and whoever else was left.

He scanned the bay. He was glad they had come here. Such a beautiful part of the world. He normally never ventured farther than the mid-Caribbean islands of Dominica and Costa Rica—he didn't have the time. But they were heading out to a full-on schedule that would last weeks, and he'd planned to squeeze every last drop of fun from the run-up to finally sealing the deal on the new polo club with Marco in the Hamptons.

All that before the big sober-up in New York with his family.

Five days until New York. The clock was ticking and his mother had been remarkably patient—for her. He'd sort that out later today—his date for the awards ceremony. There had to be *someone* he could take. Someone who would know that attending with his family didn't mean she was next on the list to join it. And that 'white tie' didn't mean turning up like a gift-wrapped Playmate. He smiled to himself. Though admittedly that held a certain appeal.

Five days. He could achieve a lot in five days. Starting with a trip on board Lord Louis's infamous *Marengo*.

He looked at it where it was berthed in the bay, dwarfing everything—like an iceberg in an ice floe of dinghies. He braced his arms on the balcony and really scanned it. He'd never been on it, but according to Raoul it was the Playboy Mansion of the seas. Well, he'd judge that for himself. Maybe. He had at least three offers tonight—and they were in the middle of nowhere.

His reputation was getting out of hand. But the oblivion of hedonism was sometimes exactly what he needed.

Tonight…? He might make an appearance and then call it a day. Though how many times had he said that? And how many times had he woken up buried underneath another blanket of limbs and loving, with another mindless, numbing headache and people wanting more than he was ever prepared to give.

He dropped his head, stared at his braced hands, white knuckles, and tensed his jaw. *Happy-go-lucky Dante.* What a sham. Like the happy family they'd show the world at the Woman of the Year Awards. A united front of high-achievers, with perfect lives and perfect partners, the Argentinian Hermidas would be honouring their American-born mother as she collected a Lifetime Award for services to charity. Charities that *didn't* begin at home, of course.

Yes, his mother would be back on the case at any moment—asking who his 'mystery date' was. The mystery was why everyone. including the press, thought he had one. He hadn't! Not yet, anyway. But he would—all he had to do was call up one of the endless stream of women they were speculating he'd bring. As long as she had an IQ above eighty and dug her own gold.

He chuckled as he recalled the list of minimum

assets his mother had rattled off when she'd first told him about tonight.

He would figure it out. He always did.

Right after he figured out what was going on over there on the *Marengo*…

He frowned, lifted his binoculars. A woman was climbing up and along the very edge of the bottom deck. A woman in a bikini. Even from this distance she was uniquely, outstandingly female. Nothing unusual in that on the *Marengo*, he supposed, but there was something strange about her.

She made her way to the side and stood completely upright on the railing. as if on the ledge of a skyscraper. waiting to jump. Tall, proud, dignified. Seconds passed. Minutes, even—and still he stared. And then, with an almost regal shake of her head, she stepped into mid-air and plunged.

God! He dropped his binoculars. She'd disappeared. Straight down into the water. No elegant dive…no playful jump. Just down like a lead pipe.

He grabbed the binoculars, paced forward. 'What the hell?'

He waited a moment, scanned the water round the yacht, but it was a shimmer of brilliant white and blue. He forced his focus as the sun needled his eyes. There was no sign of life—just the glitter and glare of heat and light. He pulled his binoculars away, rubbed at his eyes. Put them back. Nothing. Not. One. Single. Thing.

Dante paused. Surely there was nothing wrong?

Surely the people on the yacht would be on hand if something *had* happened? Surely he should mind his own business?

But he had no option. Hand on the rail, he vaulted—right over into the speedboat that was tied up as a tender. Music blasted behind him, and Raoul called his name, but he landed in front of the wheel, turned the key and was off.

The party could wait.

The boat bumped, soared and crashed over the water but he kept his gaze still and steady. What the hell had he just seen? It could just have been a dare-devil jump, but it wouldn't be the first time he had known someone try to hurt themselves...

Closer, he slowed. The last thing he should do was make the situation worse by ploughing into her.

He looked up at the *Marengo*, at its infamous majestic outline—there were people milling about, but nobody seemed to be shouting, *Man overboard!*

And then he saw her. A single pale arm like a white reed rose above the water, then lowered in a circle as she stroked the surface and moved back effortlessly.

He waited—watched, mesmerised. Each arm was raised high above her then down in a slow, graceful arc. He smiled. Put the binoculars that hung round his neck up to get a better view—he had to make sure she really was okay. She was swimming out past the safety buoys—and only a really experienced swimmer or a complete lunatic would be doing what she was doing. This was speedboat turf. Anything could go wrong.

He saw her tread water and watched for her arms to rise and circle again. For a second there was immense calm. As if time had stopped. As if all the air had been sucked from the whole wide expanse of sea and sky. And then the surface of the water churned as white limbs thrashed.

He narrowed his eyes—what had happened? She'd been gliding like a pro one minute, then thrashing like a novice the next. He powered up the boat immediately and went to her, eyes trained like a tractor beam on her. Her head sprang up and he almost felt her gaze, wide and frightened. He had to help her. There was nothing else in that moment but her safety.

He cut the engine and nosed the boat away, and then in one move dived into the water and swam with bursting lungs towards her. She was still on the surface and he reached out, grabbed her light, silky limbs and clutched them to his chest, flipping backwards and powering them on.

The frail limbs in his grasp suddenly took on a ferocious strength, and he had to dig a bit deeper to keep them afloat and moving.

'Let me go—*let me go!*' she yelled.

Shock. It had to be. But it was really not helping.

'You're fine—you're going to be okay. Relax!'

He loosened his hold and then gripped her again,

tucked his arm around her and propelled them back to his boat. She was still thrashing and yelling, and even as he reached round her waist, his hands meeting on warm wet skin, he could feel her strength and hear her rage.

A part of him fired up.

Like breaking in a new pony, he needed to overcome this flailing, furious female—pin her down and soothe her. But he had nothing to push back against, no purchase to propel her up and onto the boat. With one huge effort he raised her up and over the edge. His face caught curves and clefts, firm, soft wet skin, tiny triangles of bright green fabric and string and all sorts going on.

She landed, and leaped out of his hands as he hauled himself up and over the edge, his breath steadying into pants as he stared at this bundle of nervous energy.

She was even more beautiful up close. Her skin was pale, glistening satin, barely covered by the bikini that lay askew over lush curves. Her hair hung in soaked blonde tresses around her shoulders. Her arm… She was rubbing it up and down, up and down. He frowned as he realised just how mesmerised he was by her.

Shaking it off, he stepped towards her. 'Are you hurt?'

The look on her face…

'Am I *hurt*? You tore across the sea in this stupid boat! You nearly carved me up. *And* the marine life that actually *does* belong here—it's a miracle that I'm *not* hurt!'

Dante stared. This was beyond shock.

'I got *stung*, you stupid great idiot! That's all—there was no need for all—this.'

She stared at him, ran glinting green eyes all over him, and he felt his jaw tense, his hands flex. He found himself standing taller, puffing out his chest, staring down at her.

'No need for all what?'

He could not get this framed right in his head. She'd been struggling in the water—he was sure she had! If he hadn't seen her God knew what would have happened to her. What sort of person was ungrateful for that?

'So you didn't need any help? Well, my mistake, but you certainly didn't look like you were in control out there.'

Her head came up and she gave him that haughty look he'd clocked just before she'd vanished into the sea.

'You didn't *rescue* me! I didn't need *rescuing*! I was fine—it was only a jellyfish! And if I hadn't had to swim away from you and your stupid speedboat I would have seen it!'

Dante opened his mouth and then bit down. What a foul-tempered witch! He should have left her there. She was screaming at him when all he'd tried to do was help her.

'You might want to learn some manners, Princess. Before I toss you back overboard.'

That was exactly what he wanted to do. He could feel his shoulders tensing further and his fists bunch—he had to get himself in check. What was going on? He was easy, slow—even lazy when it came to women. He never, *ever* got fired up. Never acted without brain and body being in total harmony. Hadn't he learned anything all those years ago?

So what the hell nerve was she touching that had him flexing and puffing and grinding his jaw when he looked at her?

He looked at her now as her green eyes widened. Her rosy mouth fell open slightly, and maybe that was a moment of vulnerability stealing across her face like a cloud across the sun. Likely she was just another one of Lord Louis's cast-offs, dramatically throwing herself overboard because she'd just realised her shelf life had expired.

Who knew? Women were all games and drama. He had the T-shirt to prove it. And the only sure thing was that he was never going to be taken in by a woman again.

'Do *not* call me Princess. I do not hold that title. And you might want to *ask* people if they want to be manhandled before you chuck them onto your boat.'

'Plenty do.' Dante smiled then, and watched her eyes widen all over again. He nodded his head back to the *Sea Devil*, where the gang would be getting well back on track now. 'There's a party over there, waiting for its host to return. So if you'll excuse me…?'

He gestured to the water—jerked his thumb. She could get on with her own rescue.

'Off.'

'What?' She frowned as if he was speaking a different language—and not very clearly at that. 'Who do you think you're talking to?'

He looked round at the *Sea Devil*. Another boat was making its way towards it and now berthed alongside. He put the binoculars back up to his eyes. Looked like the Cotier sisters climbing out. He'd know those legs anywhere…

He turned back to her.

'Sorry—what?'

'You know, people like you—you *disgust* me! You're just tourists, intent on destroying this place—it's all parties and speedboats and you don't give a damn about the island, or the people, or the animals, or—'

'Maybe you didn't hear me. I said, *off*.'

Her eyes widened in shock and up went her chin even further.

'Honestly! You think you can order me around now? Really? Do you know who I am?'

'Know who you are? Apart from being the biggest pain in my ass, I couldn't care less if you were the Queen of England. Which you're not. So now I think—'

He cocked his head, relishing the pink tinge to

her neck, which seemed to be spreading to her chest. *Her chest.* She certainly had one—and it was well worth a lingering stare. But he wouldn't give her the satisfaction—even though the swell of her left breast, set almost completely free by her bikini, was quite a test.

'I think you and I have nothing left to say to one another. So I'm *ordering* you now to get off my boat.'

She stared right at him, and he knew that a lesser man would flinch. But not he. Not Dante Hermida. He might not have a doctorate from Harvard Law School, or a *Fortune 500* business like his brother—yet. But he could fight and he could ride and he could charm every woman within a hundred-mile radius.

So why was this one being so difficult?

'You've got twenty seconds. *Damn!*' he said, suddenly catching sight of the misted face of his grandfather's treasured watch.

He shook his head, held his annoyance in check. He'd nearly lost it once before over a stupid woman, but he'd managed to keep it intact for all these years—a gift from the one person on this earth who'd had time for him. Damn this woman. Standing on his boat, spraying her poison and leaving him soaked to the skin. She might look like a goddess—like some kind of deity in female form—but life was far too short to waste another second with a woman who made his hackles rise this high.

'Ten,' he said.

Biting down on the urge to throw her off himself, he ripped his T-shirt over his head and grabbed up a towel. Out of the corner of his eye he saw her watching him through narrowed eyes, seething and ungrateful. *Yeah, but there was no mistaking her hunger.* He could feel it—emanating out of every selfish pore. She might sound as if she wanted to fight, but she was eying him like a late lunch.

He patted the towel down each arm and over his pecs. 'Five.'

She was still gawping, still showing no signs of going anywhere. Slowly he grabbed each end of the towel and rubbed it across his back, then down over his abs. Finally he smoothed it over his face and dragged it roughly through his hair. Then he stood right in front of her. His shorts were soaked too. Her eyes landed there and her mouth opened on a coy, 'Oh…'

Her skin glistened in the bright late-morning light as stray droplets of water continued to course their way down all those curves. Idly he wondered if her waist-to-hip ratio was the best he'd ever seen, because it had started a reaction in his body that seemed to pay no heed at all to the fact that he really didn't like her.

It looked as if she was planning to play hardball. Okay. He was open to the idea.

Feeling more than a little turned on himself, he lifted the towel again and swiped down each leg. He had great legs—or so he was told, he thought laughingly. 'Great legs' were legs that could grip a horse, make it twist or stop with a squeeze of the thighs. But she didn't look as if riding a polo pony was what she had in mind for him.

'You don't seem to be moving, Princess. Were you hoping for some more body contact before you go?'

He was. He let his gaze travel all over her now. The twisted bikini provided *such* a generous view of her left breast. The hard bud of her nipple peeped out invitingly and he felt another hard kick of lust. For all she was annoying, she was also an incredibly attractive woman—and he could think of many ways she could redeem herself.

He cupped himself and dropped his hands to his waistband, tugged at the string and raised his eyebrows in invitation. Just how far would she let him go?

'Zero,' he said.

In one move he loosened the shorts, slid them down over his jutting erection to the wet floor of the boat and stepped out. She stood for a split second, a look of utter shock on her face, and then she spun, bolted to the side and dived off into the sea.

'Man overboard!' he called after her. 'Again.'

He felt the splash of water on his sun-warmed skin and walked to the side to see limbs and white foam as she thrashed her way back to the *Marengo*.

'Pleasure, Princess,' he said, sending her on her way with a mock salute.

Then he pulled his shorts back on and with his hand on the wheel and his foot on the floor, he powered back through the waves. If he never saw her again it would be far too soon.

CHAPTER TWO

LUCIE HEAVED HERSELF back onto the *Marengo*, wheezing and gasping and incandescent with rage. Staff appeared from every possible corner, staring at her bedraggled form, complete with purple rash. She stomped through them, flapping her arms to get them out of her way. After what she'd just been through the last thing she needed was a crowd of strangers babbling on about jellyfish stings!

Back in her quarters, she went straight into the bathroom—and it was only then that she noticed that what had started out as a hastily thrown on bikini that she'd grabbed to do a quick circuit of the yacht had now turned itself into three postage stamps of ill-positioned fabric.

She turned herself this way and that in the mirror, looking to see what he had seen. And it wasn't good—the ten pounds she had lost certainly hadn't gone from her boobs or her bottom.

She pulled the skimpy thing off and tossed it in the laundry basket, wondering if she would ever have the nerve to wear it again. Then she stepped into the shower and let the hot water course down over her. What on earth would happen next on this disastrous day?

All she'd wanted when she'd jumped in was a relaxing, calming swim to clear her head, and then she'd planned a bath and an hour or so with the hairstylist and the beauty therapist to help her prepare for tonight. But instead of an aromatherapy massage and pampering to within an inch of her life she'd been nearly ploughed to death by a speedboat and stung by a jellyfish—not to mention that whole encounter on the boat.

She shuddered and reached for the shampoo. So much for being relaxed. She'd have to deal with her social anxiety on top of all the other anxieties she'd developed so far today. One thing was sure—she was in for hours of deep breathing until she finally put her head on her pillow tonight.

Damn that stupid man and his stupid boat!

And his *outrageous* behaviour.

She let the soap run free and stared down at her body, cringing because he had seen so much of it. But, even though she might not have been exactly dressed for an audience with Her Majesty, that didn't excuse his unashamedly egotistical actions! Standing there in those red swim-shorts, with his manhood outlined so clearly...

She shook her head and scrubbed at the jellyfish sting like Lady Macbeth, as if by trying to get rid of the mark she would get rid of the image of him. The look that he'd speared her with—that supercilious grin and those twin dimples, those bright blue eyes that had mocked her. Those shoulders and those impossibly firm, smooth pectorals. An actual six-pack that one could imagine—*touching...*

What an arrogant, egotistical, boneheaded...

Urgh!

At least this was one thing that she and her mother agreed on. Men who were so *obvious* about sex were normally more to be pitied than despised. And he was definitely obvious! And she *totally* despised him.

Who was she kidding? She knew absolutely zero about men and even less about sex. One didn't really fall over them at home with the governess or at an all-girls boarding school. Thankfully.

The last thing she wanted was a life like her mother's—diets and dresses, reporters and snappers. With every last move scrutinised and analysed and published for the world to see. And having to wear that *everything's fabulous, darling* face everywhere she went—even if she'd just caught her husband cheating or her weight had ricocheted to above eight stone.

It wasn't that she was vehemently opposed to men—but they had very little to recommend them.

Take this yacht, for example. It was such a drain on the family finances when they could be funding more eco projects, out here or at home. But her father simply *had* to have it so that he could 'entertain'.

She flipped the taps off and stepped out of the

shower, twisting her hair up into a turban and grabbing a towel as she went.

Her father's answer to everything was to throw money at it. He'd paid for the food, the drink, the staff, her dress, the harbour fees and the biggest auction item—the use of his yacht for a month.

But his most generous gift, as far as she was concerned, was that he had stayed away—as instructed. It would be a disaster to end all if he suddenly turned up. She'd seen first-hand what happened to women under the age of ninety whenever he was near—and it wasn't a pretty sight. No wonder she'd found that man today so irritating. He was just a young, blond version of her father. All ego, all sex appeal—and disaster written all over him.

She began searching for something to cool her skin, but really there wasn't enough coconut oil in the whole of the Caribbean to smooth away the vicious red marks from the jellyfish sting—or the mental scarring from her encounter with that—that lunatic on a speedboat!

She checked her phone, registering that the blank screen meant her mother was now even less likely to put in an appearance.

She put it down with a sigh and lifted a pot of her most expensive unguent. She dropped a thick, gloopy dollop onto her palm, spreading it across her arm and chest where the jellyfish sting now bloomed like a cheap tattoo. But it still didn't look any better. And she had less than an hour now until she had to squeeze herself into that hideously revealing frock and face those hideously overbearing crowds—completely alone.

Another wave of nausea announced itself and she swallowed quickly, lest any more acid land in her mouth.

Its lid screwed back on, she replaced the little pot on the dressing table and stared at herself in the mirror, suddenly noticing that lights were starting to appear in the harbour, announcing the evening ahead. And here was she—stressed, not dressed, and with no mother in sight to take over the horrific task of hostessing.

Maybe she could 'have a migraine'. She'd always thought it such a convenient ailment. How could anyone prove it one way or another? She could feign some sort of illness and let the whole thing look after itself. The conservation centre staff would be there. Somebody was bound to be willing to host…

She wanted to scream into a pillow, but this was her mess and there was nothing else to do but to get on with it. It was bad enough that the guests thought they were going to be schmoozing with Lady Viv— who now only just might be persuaded to put in an appearance on camera—so Lucie certainly couldn't leave the whole thing to anyone else.

She ran to the bathroom. This nausea was overwhelming. She had to get it under control—one way or another.

CHAPTER THREE

LUCIE CLUTCHED A glass of fortifying champagne between white-knuckled fingers and stood like one of the pillars on the mid-deck. Any minute now someone might drape a piece of muslin over her and tie a balloon round her neck.

Her first glass had been half emptied in a single gulp in her room, which had led to a choking fit and a grave look from the hairstylist, who had been packing up her stuff. She'd better not start throwing alcohol down her neck—even though she'd run out of ideas for a quick and painless death. A little deadly nightshade—how did that work?—or something one could simply inhale or swallow. And then she'd fold like a chimney struck by a wrecking ball, while all these strangers continued to sip obliviously on their champagne.

They were arriving all the time. She could hear them, smell them, see them—one big, sensory blur. Her face felt tight—was she even smiling? She had no idea—couldn't feel anything other than the hammer of her heart and the flush of burning red that still bloomed across her chest and neck. She tried to open her mouth to say hello, but the word stuck in her throat, died there.

All she could do was stand there—shoulders back, stomach in, chest out—with her glass clutched in her hand and her face stretched into what she hoped was a smile. All she could do was breathe deeply and wait for it to be over.

'I haven't seen Lady Vivienne yet—is she here?'

The Mexican Wave of those words washed over her every few minutes. If she heard it one more time she might actually throw herself overboard. That would be quite dramatic. Lucie ran a mental image as another crowd of people who, like her mother, probably couldn't tell the difference between a turtle and a tortoise, came trundling onto the yacht, making too much noise.

Suddenly the Mexican Wave turned back on itself. Bodies seemed to wheel around and preen and pose and Lucie's heart began to pound even more loudly.

Someone interesting was arriving. Someone very interesting.

Could it be…? Could it *possibly* be…? Had her mother actually dropped everything back home and got on a jet to get here? Maybe she had heard the hurt and felt some kind of empathy or love or even just motherly duty towards her. Was that possible?

She turned with the crowd and strained her head to see. Everybody was thronging towards the steps. It *had* to be her. Who else would get this level of interest in a crowd that was already chock-full of the so-called 'it-list'?

Maybe she had been too harsh? Too quick to judge? She hadn't really given her a proper chance to explain. She had said she would come for part of it—hadn't she? And *she* had been the one to plan most of the party—who'd laid down all those rules. And they'd really, really made Lucie focus. She did like the fact that she could see past her stomach to her feet now. And it felt good—it really did—that she could tolerate the heat so much more easily and not worry about her thighs rubbing together when she walked.

Yes, she had her mother to thank for all that—and she would. That *was* her, wasn't it? Coming aboard? Strange that she hadn't come in on the helipad, but maybe she'd found a different way to get here. Maybe that was what she'd been about to say on the phone before she'd cut her off so abruptly.

Lucie finally found a space in the crowd and got ready to greet her. But…where was she? There was no sign of Lady Vivienne. No gleaming perfect smile or couture-perfect outfit. No. There, strolling towards her, was another version of perfection. The male version. Dark blond hair flopped over an eye, golden skin, bluest, truest gaze and the laziest, most indolent grin.

The idiot from the boat.

What on earth was everyone doing, staring at him? Lucie looked to her left and right. And what on earth was he doing *here*?

Suddenly her dry voice formed words and actually delivered them.

'Who invited you?'

He was strolling towards her as if he could barely find the energy, but her words had an effect. Oh, yes.

He straightened and his shoulders went back—rigid just for a moment, but no mistaking it. Exactly the same way he'd looked on his boat earlier, when she'd had the temerity to question his intelligence. When he'd seemed made of steel and stone.

And then he slipped back into that easy, breezy, nothing-is-a-problem attitude.

'Invited? You mean begged, don't you?'

Lucie fumed. The big idiot was standing right in front of her now. On either side of him stood two pull-up banners—sea turtles swimming, with white lettering clearly displaying the name of her foundation: Caribbean Conservation Centre.

'Not if you were the last man alive! This is for people who're trying to do something to save endangered animals. You probably can't even *spell* endangered!'

He looked at her, tucked one hand on his hip—and her eye slid *there* again! Despite herself. His perfect wide shoulders, broad, strong chest and narrow waist were all tucked up inside a soft blue shirt the colour of his eyes. Not that she particularly cared about his eyes. Or how arresting they were. Or how hard it was to look away.

'Maybe you can find someone to play schools with later, Princess.' He was looking down at her as if he had some other kind of game in mind. 'But you don't have a monopoly on helping save the planet. I'm sure my friends' money is quite as good as everybody else's.'

Lucie slid her eyes around to see the party he'd come with all disappearing into the crowd. She knew she should get over her disappointment towards her mother and her anger towards him and find someone out there who could run the auction. But his very presence riled her.

'You have *friends*? How did you get them— kidnapping them? Throwing them onto your boat?'

'Trust me, kidnapping you couldn't be further from my mind.'

He slipped her a self-important smile, bared a flash of teeth between two proud dimples.

She could sense the crowd getting fuller, the time coming closer. Suddenly the realisation of where she was and who she was and what she was supposed to be doing overwhelmed her.

An anxious voice to her right told her there were only twenty minutes until the auction. Followed by yet another question about her mother. Followed by a third question about who exactly was going to announce the items if not Lady Vivienne... Were they to assume that Lady Lucinda would be doing it in her stead?

She hadn't sorted anything out. She had buried

her head, hoping the problem would just solve itself. That a miracle would happen. But it hadn't.

The faces around her were all staring. People began to crush in. Her personal space was disappearing, and with it the air to breathe. And still he stood, right in front of her, with that dimpled smile plastered all over his face, that supercilious look dripping contempt.

'Lady Lucinda…? We need to get started now. Will you…?'

She turned, and a sickening grey mist swept down over her vision. A hand moved, sweeping out to show her where she should proceed. Blindly she moved ahead, her eyes focused on the little podium that had been built up at the head of the ballroom.

To its left and right were the various objects and artefacts that had been gifted by her mother and her coterie of high society friends who had been persuaded to be part of this. A couture gown here…a handbag there… Jewellery, silk scarves, cosmetics and more. A week on someone's island in the Indian Ocean…a fortnight at an English country house in the shooting season. A signed polo shirt and tickets to a match in Dubai…

Dazedly she realised that *that* was who he was— the polo player. The one her mother had practically passed out over when she'd heard he'd be coming. The one who was an *'utter Lothario'*.

But what did any of that matter now? Her mother

wasn't here and she was—and she had to step up, get on with this auction. She *had* to.

She stared again at the tables set up with all the goodies. She could list each and every one. She had typed them into the programme that she'd sent out, into the advertising copy she'd placed in various local and international publications—she knew every single thing and who had donated it.

But there was no way she would be able to say that. Say anything at all. Her voice was buried under a rock of anxiety.

There was nothing she could do—*nothing* she could do. The suffocating fear built, the tightness returned, and the terror of being right here, right now, became excruciating. She looked for one of the staff from the conservation centre. She scanned the room, but all she could see was the crushing crowd of people, hovering and staring. They were all around her, gawping as if she were some kind of crazy. Which she was.

She had to get out—had to get out or she'd pass out.

'Hey, what's going on?'

She could see jewel-bright colours, dresses,, jewellery, glasses… She could hear voices, feel the daggers of their derision.

'Hey.'

A warm, strong hand wrapped around her arm. She jumped at the sudden contact and tried to jerk away, but the sickness was overwhelming.

'Get your hands off me,' she whispered.

'Slow down, Princess. You trying to take some-one's eye out?'

Lucie slowed…stopped. He was right behind her, his hand still on her arm. Her skin, clammy now, felt the chill of the night breeze and the warmth of his touch. She reached out, tried to lay her hand on the railing—missed. She stepped forward, unsee-ing, stumbled…

'Steady on. Stand still.'

She grasped the rail and stood staring down at the black sea. Her stomach still heaved, but the spin-ning had stopped and the whirling grey settled as the world became centred around a solid warm wall behind her, stabilising her. A large male body. He laid one hand beside hers on the rail and placed the other at her neck, weighted and heavy, and for once she didn't flinch.

'This is the last thing I want to be doing, but you look as if you're about to pass out.'

She felt the warmth seep through her. Her freezing skin was suddenly soothed, enveloped and wrapped up in another human's body. How many times had she been held like this? Ever? Never?

Could she remember a time when the touch of an-other had been accepted, never mind encouraged? No. She wasn't the type. The Bonds did not hug each other—never mind strangers.

She pushed away from him—put her hands against the solidity and shoved hard as she could.

'Get off me—go away.' Her voice came out like a hiss.

He stepped back, hands up in mock surrender. Her eyes flashed to his face and she caught a look of surprise.

'No problem.'

'Ladies and gentlemen, the auction is about to begin. Can you please take your places in the salon?'

'No problem at all—and believe me when I tell you this: there won't be a third time.'

'Can Lady Lucinda please make her way to the podium for the start of tonight's charity auction? So many wonderful items for such a wonderful cause.'

The voice, like a call to the gates of hell, boomed out across the Tannoy.

'I can't...' she breathed to the wind. 'I simply can't...'

He turned. The blue shirt, broad back, warmth and strength moved away, and she knew that there really was no way out.

'Me either,' he said, and he was stepping away, leaving her in the grip of the suffocating black velvet night and the sickening dread of the sea of up-turned, staring faces.

'Please...' she said, reaching him, grabbing for his arm.

He turned immediately, glancing down at the hand that gripped his elbow.

'What?'

She opened her mouth, looked over his shoulder.

The tinny voice boomed out again, calling people forward, making some kind of apology about her mother's lack of appearance. Her fingers gripped his arm. Pressed into his flesh.

'I've got to say, Princess, you're sending out some *very* conflicting signals. So allow me to be clear...'

He put his hand over hers and slowly began to prise her fingers up.

The voice sounded again. Everyone was in position. She *had* to do this. She had to locate her breath, count in and out slowly, and then she'd be fine. She would be absolutely fine.

Her fingers, now free of his arm, hung in mid-air like a wizened claw.

'I can't go in there. I can't be in front of all those people.'

He stepped back into her space, blotting out the view. 'You can't be in front of all those people? Hang on—is this *your* party? Are *you* Lady Lucinda?'

She clenched her eyes and nodded.

He looked behind him, as if expecting to see something horrifying, then turned back to face her. 'What's going on? Is this some kind of emotional blackmail?'

She could barely breathe now, the panic had gripped her so fiercely.

'It's the auction,' she gasped.

'You're telling me *that's* what's got you like this? Is that what this is all about? Really? The auction?'

He was staring at her as if she was deranged. Which was exactly how she felt.

'You might have thought of that *before* you organised it, then, wouldn't you say?'

She nodded, swallowed, put her hand on her chest and tried hard to slow her furious heartbeat.

'Just another example of your consideration for others? Impressive. Awesome. You really *are* something else, Princess.'

And he turned on his heel.

'No—no, you can't. Please!' Lucie heard herself begging and saw herself reach out, grab his arm, pull him back. She really pulled him back.

He turned. Looked down at her, hands on hips.

'Please? Please, what? What do you expect me to do? Help you? Are you serious? After the way you've acted?'

'I can't go in there.' Her voice was little more than a whisper. 'I simply can't.'

She didn't know herself what she expected him to do. All she knew was that for some reason his presence, his body—whatever it was—she felt warmed by it. And when she felt warm she was less likely to run away—or in this case swim away.

He turned to look at the room full of people. Restless people.

'All these good people here are waiting patiently for you to go in there and start this off, aren't they?'

Lucie nodded, held her head in her hands.

'And you're in no fit state to deliver. Are you?'

Her shoulders drooped as she shook her head. What an idiot she was. A gauche idiot with social anxiety as an extra talent.

Suddenly she felt her chin being lifted up.

'Is it nerves? Is that it? You're stressed out because your mother hasn't turned up and suddenly the spotlight's on you?'

She heard him murmur the words. Someone understood. Someone genuinely understood. How many times had she tried to explain to the people close to her that she simply couldn't do the things they could? How many times had she heard the word 'nonsense' fired at her? And how many times had she seen her mother sweep past her, shaking her head and rolling her eyes, making her feel such an abject, worthless piece of garbage just because she wasn't like her?

'God only knows why I'd do anything other than get as far away from you as possible, but I don't suppose it would kill me to help you out. And I can't really stand back and watch you let all those people down...'

She stared up into that face. It was suddenly serious, the dimples subsumed into all that beautiful golden skin. His eyes were grave. And she felt again that strange sense of caring, of kindness, of being anchored.

Lucie nodded. She stood in the shelter of his warm, strong body and nodded.

He looked at her for a long second, then stepped away, shaking his head.

'God only knows...'

She watched his back as he walked into the crowd, her breaths lengthening and her heart gradually steadying. Easy and lazy—no problem at all for him to go and stand before a crowd, all eyes trained on him.

Lucie's gaze fixed on the breadth of his shoulders, the slight swing of his backside, so fabulously formed inside those trousers, the angle of each leg as he stepped so damn nonchalantly onto the podium, before the crowd of women who clearly thought exactly the same as she did closed over his path like waves of hungry harpies.

She might have solved one problem, but she had the feeling she had launched herself head-first into another.

CHAPTER FOUR

SHE WAS OUT there on the deck, watching. He could feel her stare from time to time. He searched for that shimmer of green satin, or the glint of her golden hair. But there were far too many people in the room, pledging their money for things they really didn't need, and he was working them as if his life depended on getting them to bid for each and every one of these glamorous trinkets.

When his own prize came up—the holiday in Dubai and tickets to the race day his team would be riding in—the air was electric. Of course it helped that he was there, and flirting with every one of those women, some of whom he was pretty sure he might have flirted with before. Maybe he'd even done more than flirt, but tonight, for sure, he only had eyes for Lady Lucinda Bond —'Princess' to him.

He saw her pass along the back of the salon, deckside. She looked as if she was back in the game—her shoulders were down and her chin was high. Her face was side-lit, but only flashes of those proud features appeared through the rows of women who waved their paddles at him. He knew he should leave well alone, but he was going to track her down as soon as the last item was sold—if only to give her the chance to apologise and to thank him.

He was feeling pretty good, to be fair. It wasn't every day you got the chance to help raise two and a half million US dollars for charity. She should be stoked. So her glamorous mother hadn't turned up? No bad thing as far as Dante could see. She came across as a bit self-obsessed anyway.

He exited the salon to a round of applause and several slaps on the back and kisses on the cheek. That was all he was offering.

Night on deck was thick and black, but the trail of the moon across the water that separated the *Marengo* from the *Sea Devil* was a silvery carpet of light topped with a veil of blinking stars. Even *he* couldn't help but be struck by the prettiness of the scene, by the twinkling and bobbing of buoys and lights and the fairytale island of Petit Pierre in the background.

He rounded the deck, staring in at the other rooms that held the usual party suspects. Drink was flowing and chat was getting easier. On he moved, pausing at a tiny sweep of steps that led to a dance floor and a pulsating beat where bodies moved in time to the music. He scanned it. A few people waved him over. Friends. Raoul, for one. He'd join them shortly—as soon as he'd tracked down Her Ladyship.

They looked to be having a great time—there

were some new faces, new bodies, and Raoul looked as if he was already predating on them. Normally that alone would have been enough to spur him on—the competition, the hunt. He glanced back, held up his hand—five minutes. Raoul grinned.

Someone in front of him turned. A blonde, about five seven, slim and sure, her long hair in a knot on top of her head.

Dante froze.

It couldn't be.

A familiar sickening chill seeped through his body. It had been so long since he had felt that—*so* long. The cast of that jawline, the angle of that cheekbone…

But of course it couldn't be. There were no such things as ghosts.

Still, he was rooted to the spot. A body bumped his, someone else spoke, yet another person touched his arm. He jerked it away angrily as he stared at the profile, waiting for her to turn, waiting for his eyes to tell him what his rational brain knew were the facts. The dead didn't come back to life. And Celine di Rosso was well and truly dead. Hadn't she made sure *he* would be the one to find her, after all?

Raoul was frowning. Tipping his chin up in question. The conversation stopped. The woman turned herself right around. Right around to face Dante.

The face of a stranger. The same angle of the jaw, hollow of those cheekbones, the same long neck and knot of blonde hair—but at least twenty years younger than Celine. Even thinking those words was like succumbing to the sickness again.

He blinked and the woman smiled. Raoul waved him over. And then he felt pressure on his arm again.

'Señor Hermida?'

He turned and there she was. Lady Lucie. He came to as if he'd been out cold—as if she were standing there with smelling salts instead of a rigid arm held out in front for some kind of ceremonial handshake.

Her outline formed in the haze of long-ago horror that had descended all around him. He felt his smile slide back into place—more easily than he would ever have imagined, having just seen that doppelgänger. He could see her features. He scanned her. She looked questioningly at him and he knew he must look as if he'd been bludgeoned, or worse.

She was tight-mouthed, but she looked a damn sight better than when he'd last spoken to her. She hadn't been pretending, that was for sure—that had been a panic attack if ever he'd seen one. And, hell, he'd seen more than a few. What on earth her own demons were was anyone's guess, but he knew better than anyone that all was rarely as it seemed.

'Princess?' he replied, watching her eyes drifting to the smile that he knew warmed even the hardest of hearts.

She flashed her eyes right up into his and scowled. 'I know you're doing that simply to annoy me, but for the last time may I ask that when you use a title you use the correct one?'

He bowed, Walter Raleigh–style. 'Yes. Whatever Your Ladyship says.'

He would have sworn she almost stamped her feet underneath the satin shimmer of the dress that skimmed down her body and even now had his hands twisting out of the bunched fists and flexing with the unspent touch of her. She had spirit. In spades. And it was back in abundance.

'What I said was thank you,' she delivered in clipped, sharp tones, and she tilted her nose up, as if he had come to the main entrance when he really should be using the servants' door.

'Thank you?'

She looked flustered now. But she was back to acting the princess and he'd be damned if he was going to let her wriggle away that easily.

'Yes, thank you. For…you know…stepping up…'

Dante took a step back, let his smile do the work, let his eyes trail all over her the way he wanted to trail his hands. The glorious spill of her breasts, scooped and positioned for a man just to release into his hands, to tease with his mouth. The shoulders curved gently, the hips swelled from that tiny waist. She was a feast, a banquet, an image of woman he had rarely, if ever, seen before.

But she was trying to pull rank with him, and he for one was not going to play ball in that particular game of ego.

'So, yes. Thank you. It…er…seems to have been a success.'

He watched a fan of colour seep all over her creamy chest and this time he didn't move his eyes. She was too tempting, on so many different levels. And, yes, maybe seeing that image of Celine had aroused his passion, raised his ire, but he was going to make her apologise over and over again—and thank him in ways she'd never even dreamed of.

'Lots of happy people back there, Princess, yes.' She scowled.

'And it was for them that I did it. I hate to see people getting short-changed when their expectations have been raised. You know, in a way it was a bit of a rescue situation... I saw someone in trouble and I dropped everything—and I mean *everything*—put my foot to the floor, put myself out there. I mean, what do I know about auctions?'

He lanced her with a stare and watched as her eyes widened like saucers. Then he gave her a little wink and a smile. She was thinking. She knew exactly what he meant and she was reliving those moments. The pretty pink bloom shifted further from her glorious cleavage to the column of her neck.

'Is that where the jellyfish got you?' he asked, nodding to the scattering of the rash all over her beautiful chest.

She looked down, then up. Opened her mouth. Looked even more embarrassed. He could let her off the hook now, but she really *had* been incredibly rude. And he really *was* incredibly angry.

'I...I...'

He leaned in to her space, and her eyes widened even further as she leaned back. Then he placed a finger on her lips.

'Shh, Princess. It's okay. Apology accepted. I was happy to help out.'

He lifted his finger from the moist, soft pillow of her lips before he gave in to the temptation to slide it right inside and have her suck it. He tilted her chin up instead and leaned forward—just a tiny inch, just close enough to scent the luxury and the class that oozed from her pores. He lingered there, savouring in equal measure her surprise and her femininity. Letting her get caught up in the moment of thinking that he just might kiss her.

His hand slid out, all by itself, and lightly skimmed her waist. And just like that he felt her melt—felt all those thorns wilt and fall like petals to his feet. He nodded to her, telling her with a wink that he knew she was moments away from giving in completely.

And then he stepped back. 'Really, I was happy to help—it was no problem at all.'

He slipped her a smile and let his hand slide off the side of her hip. She was hot. For him. *Oh, yes.*

He walked away.

'Wait! I mean…' She was literally pulling on his sleeve now.

He stopped. Raoul was watching closely, raising a shot glass with the others in his little circle of new blood, and downing it to a chorus of cheers.

Dante waited, then turned as slowly as he could, savouring every last moment.

'You mean *what*, Princess?'

He glanced at her, one eyebrow raised in a jaunty, light-hearted way that belied every last emotion that coursed through his veins like trails of lit gasoline.

'Okay, I'm sorry for the things I said earlier. I realise now that you were only trying to help. And thanks—thank you for then, and for now. You really…got me out of a hole.'

'Forget it,' he said, and moved away.

She moved with him. He felt the hand on his arm.

'Look, let me make it up to you.'

Perfect, thought Dante, silently high-fiving himself, aware of the scrutiny from Raoul.

'Okay,' he said slowly. 'Did you have something in mind?'

He turned right around now—slowly—moved ever so slightly back into her space, watched the telltale signs spill across her face.

'Would you care to join me for a drink?'

She turned hopeful green eyes on him and he smiled softly. She was like a moist, plump peach, ripened on a tree and just about to fall into his hands. But sometimes the fruits that looked the sweetest were the ones that tasted toxic. He knew that better than anyone.

There was something about Lady Lucie that made him pause. He could so easily take her to bed…give her a night she'd never forget. And then what? Another night? There were only a few days before he had to head east. He didn't want anything lasting with anyone. Even if their chemistry *was* good—and, yes, there was every indication that it would be—even if they stayed in bed for the next four days it would all end as it always did. With his *Hey, it's been great* chat.

The last thing he wanted was any drama whatsoever. And this one had 'starring role' in lights all around her. He needed release, yes—but not with someone as emotional as she. That was one script he didn't want to read ever again.

He cupped her shoulder, gave it a soft rub.

'Thanks, Princess. Another time, maybe.'

He didn't wait to see how she took that—he just moved on. He was going to split...head into town and sort out his head. Ghosts required exorcism, and he was itching to start.

CHAPTER FIVE

LUCIE WATCHED HIM lope off with that overtly sexual athleticism she found so fascinating.

What on earth…? Talk about reading someone wrong. She'd been sure he was interested in her—much more than she was in him. In fact less than twelve hours ago she hadn't even known his name, far less given him this amount of headspace. She actually shook her head to see if she could clear him out of it. But since the nausea and breathlessness had dissipated as she'd watched him own the auction, she'd found him creeping inside it—images of him and his golden smile and sinful body. He'd wowed the crowd…in fact she was sure he'd done a much better job than her mother could ever have done. And part of her longed for her to know that.

Right on cue, one of the staff indicated to her across the room. *Phone. Lady Vivienne.* Lucie felt her shoulders tense again and her fists fill with handfuls of the satin of her dress. But she had no option.

She made her way across the room, smiling stiffly at those who greeted her.

'Hello, Mother.'

'Lucie, what on earth is going on?'

'How's Simon? Much recovered? All trouble sorted?'

'You know it's rude to answer a question with a question. I can only assume you've been drinking, Lucie, because I can't for the life of me think of any other reason why you'd be acting like this.'

'I'm sorry, Mother. Shall we start again? You were asking what on earth is going on. We've just made over two and a half a million dollars for the charity. That's what's going on.'

'You know perfectly well what I'm talking about. This was the ideal opportunity for you to sort out those silly panic attacks and you didn't even try.'

Lucie was stunned. 'You surely don't mean to tell me that you set me up like this on *purpose*?'

'I didn't say that,' her mother answered stiffly, 'but it was a perfect opportunity wasted.'

'Sorry, Mother, but I had to make a decision to prevent five hundred guests being bitterly disappointed. Dante Hermida—the polo player—offered, and I think we—*he*—actually did a really good job!'

She wouldn't rub her mother's nose in it. Of course not. But she was desperately keen for her to hear just how well they'd done.

'"A really good job"? Let me be clear, Lucinda. First of all I learn that you stood in the middle of that classless great boat like a gibbering jelly, and then—worse—you actually passed the gavel to *Dante Hermida*, of all people! That utter Lothario? Didn't I warn you to stay well away from men like that? This very afternoon? And then you substitute him for me and are seen hanging all over him. Have you no shame? I thought I'd brought you up to be better than that. I absolutely forbid you to have any more to do with him—do you hear me? Lucinda?'

Lucie stared at the patterns she was drawing on the mink velvet carpet with the pointed toe of her shoe. Then she examined her nails. They were flawless—lovely, actually—and she thought she might keep the polish on past tomorrow morning. Perhaps. She pressed her lips together to see if the stickiness from the gloss was still there, but of course the last thing that had been there had been Dante's finger.

She dropped her head back and let the phone slide to her neck, where she cradled it in against her skin—anything to drown out the sound of her mother's unstinting whingeing. Brought her up? If it weren't so sad it would be funny. The house mistress and the nanny had brought her up. Her mother and father had been far too busy living their own lives to bother with anything as inconvenient as a child.

A tray of champagne passed by at just the right moment and she snagged a glass. Her second of the night. She was learning to enjoy it—and it slid down easily. More easily than usual, since she knew her mother would disapprove so heartily.

'I have to go, Mother. Thank you so much for calling, but my guests need me.'

'Guests? I hope you don't mean that polo player? I'm warning you, Lucinda—do you hear me? Stay away...'

'Actually, Mother—that's exactly who I mean. And this time I'm going to make a proper job of it.'

She didn't wait to say goodbye. She stared at the phone heard the whining, appalling voice of her mother—her *own* mother—still screeching at her. She clicked it off and dropped it in an ice bucket.

She was too far gone for tears—too wrung out, too exhausted. If she ever had a daughter she would never, *ever* say or do the hurtful, horrid things her mother did. She would nurture her child, love her and care for her. She would protect her from harm, but make her strong enough to stand up on her own two feet.

She'd had enough. Totally had enough. All those weeks and months of diet, of exercise, of listening to her mother's 'rules' and her stress about her 'real' family. She didn't give a damn about the success of the night, or the money they raised. She didn't give a damn about anything other than herself!

Well, she might think she could lay down the law from three thousand miles away, and tell her who she could see and what she could do, but there was no way she was going to let herself be dictated to like that. The hypocrisy was outrageous. All these years of listening to her rant about men suddenly crystallised into one clear thought—*why?* What was so bad about them? Why was her mother so animated when it came to her rules about men?

For the second time Lucie made her way through rooms full of people laughing and drinking, but this time she held her head up. Rage was her engine, and she knew it. She didn't glance left or right, just focused on moving swiftly through the crowd. She'd get off the yacht, so that the staff didn't have to be put on the spot the next time her mother called. Someone had been grilled by her mother before she'd called her. Someone had told her all about her moments with Dante.

Dante!

The one man she had been warned to stay away from. And the one man she felt incredibly compelled to seek out right now.

He was interested in her—she knew he was. All she had to do was act a little less like a blubbering idiot and a little more like the sophisticates he was used to.

She owed it to herself to try...

The *Marengo* was moored on the busiest stretch of the harbour, directly opposite the chicest nightclub on the island. Dante stood a moment on the jetty, watching the lines of partygoers queuing along the front. He could feel the 'good times' tension in the air—could feel it in his own body. He knew exactly how this evening was going to roll. It was like a drug to him—a few beers, a few laughs, women flirting, he taking his time, then the after-party, then the aftermath of that.

Pure. Unadulterated. Oblivion.

He reassured himself every time that everyone else was praying to the same gods in this particular church. That way there was no guilt. No need for confession.

He couldn't remember ever caring about the motivations of any romantic partner before, but he was pretty sure that Lady Lucinda didn't shake what her mama gave her every weekend, like some of the rest of that set. Good-time girls were just that. And he wasn't fool enough to ignore the fact that for many of them it was all a big act. A big hook with which they landed their catch.

But he had never bitten yet. Never would. Lose his unlimited pass to oblivion? Get mired in a relationship? Smoke and mirrors—that was all happy relationships were. He didn't begrudge anyone their 'lifetime partner', if that was what they wanted to call it, but he didn't believe the hype.

Seeing that Celine body double tonight had shaken him up—he had to admit it. But there had been a time when it would have taken him a lot longer to calm down. Back in his late teens, when it had still been a raw wound. Back then he would have been laid out for days on a self-destructive path. Now he was fine. He had more important things to worry about than something that had happened all those years ago. He'd learned to switch off, to deal with it.

He just hoped tonight would be one of those nights where he found the switch easily.

He looked along the front of the black glass building at the outdoor lounge area. Tall white tables and bar stools. Parasols and potted palms. Ice buckets and cocktails. Women wearing very little. Some of them beautiful, some of them hot. But as his gaze skimmed back and forth he found it hovering even longer on the jetty. He felt strangely underwhelmed by the whole thing. There really was nothing he was remotely interested in pursuing—nothing enticing him to step into that particular haven.

He wanted fire. He wanted passion. He wanted beauty.

Class.

And he was beginning to think that there was only woman who was going to do it for him. If he got the chance a second time he doubted he would be able to say no.

'Hello, there! I thought it was you.'

Dante heard the perfectly pronounced vowels and knew his deal was sealed.

He turned away from the crowd. 'Party over?'

She was truly lovely. He let his eyes slide and savour. Her hair fell in long waves, skimming over those shoulders, lying in inviting silken folds over her cleavage. He took his time. He had no wish to hurry as he relearned every soft curve, felt himself become aroused, welcomed it.

'Only I thought it was good etiquette for the hostess to stay until the last guest had left?'

She blushed in that haughty, *how-dare-you?* manner and he felt a grin spread out across his face. The corner of her mouth twitched up and her eyes danced in answer, but still she held herself aloft and aloof.

She was here, she'd come after him, but she was going to make him work. He got that.

Wind skimmed around them, causing the hem of her dress to rise. The fabric clung to her long legs, outlining slim calves and the flare of incredibly feminine hips. His eyes dropped to the soft V between her legs and his arousal kicked up another gear as the shimmery satin outlined her mound. A long slow breath of approval escaped through his lips and he raised his eyes to hers in approbation.

She accepted it.

'As far as I am concerned, you *are* the party.'

She spoke quietly, but he didn't miss the shiver of hesitation.

'You've really thought this through?'

He owed her one more lifeline. Because something told him that when she fell—as they all did—she was going to fall headfirst.

'Because you don't want to wake up with your head on the wrong pillow.'

'I want to wake up with my head on *your* pillow,' she said.

'Is that so?' he asked, stepping a little closer. He watched, becoming more and more aware that her regal act was just that—she was not quite so in command as she liked to portray. 'That's some honour you're bestowing—and with that honour comes responsibility, should I accept it...'

He took another step, and she leaned back ever so slightly before straightening herself up. He watched her perfect throat as she swallowed, the movement in her skin drawing his eye, inflaming his blood. *Oh, yes.*

'Well...' she breathed, and the sound disappeared into the slap of water on the sides of the jetty and the bustle and buzz of the night all around them. 'Do you accept?'

'What exactly are you offering, Princess?'

'As soon as you drop that stupid moniker I might tell you.'

Dante laughed as he closed the gap. They stood almost toe to toe. And this time she leaned back only to look up at him. She was getting into her stride now and he was loving it.

'You don't need to tell me anything. I can see it written all over you. In giant neon letters.'

Her eyes flashed and darted over his face.

'Is that so?' she asked, repeating his words, mocking him. 'We have our little spelling test after all.'

And then he grinned, and she grinned, and he put his hands on her waist, exactly where he had wanted to rest them all evening. They fitted nicely in the soft curves. He tugged her to him. Her hands jerked up in a defensive movement but they landed gently on his chest. He looked down as she spread her fingers wide.

'What exactly is it,' she began, lifting her eyes in a coy little move as old as time, 'that I'm spelling out for you?'

Dante stepped a little closer. He took his hands from her waist and skimmed them up over her ribs with immense restraint, feather-light. He slowly brushed the sides of her breasts, her shoulders, and then gently cupped her jaw. He trailed his fingers over her cheeks and gently drew a circle round each eye.

'With these bewitching eyes, you're showing me every single thought that's going on in here.' He tapped her brow. 'And those thoughts are…' He leaned in, took a breath beside her ear, and whispered, 'Dirty.'

She shivered. He heard it and he saw it. Then she closed her eyes, and he knew that he was as hard as he'd ever been. She was going to be delicious.

He moved to her other ear. She flinched but he held her steady.

'You have a very filthy mind, Lucie,' he whispered, and she shuddered right there in his arms.

It was all he could do not to grind himself against her. One or two people had passed by and they were just in sight of the queue of partygoers. He was going to have to exercise huge restraint. *Huge*.

'You're bluffing,' she breathed back. 'You think everyone thinks like you.'

'Is that right?'

He kept his mouth right beside her ear, an inch above it. A warm, sweet smell—*her* warm, sweet smell—wound up and he breathed it in. She melted against him, stretched her neck out for him, and he let his lips graze the satiny skin all the way down to her collar.

'Mmm, Lucie... What do you think I'm thinking right now?'

Her hands were still lying across his chest, getting in the way of what he wanted. He lifted first one hand, then the other, and she wound them round the back of his neck. He looked down at her upturned face. She was undone, but she was pulling herself together. He had to hand it to her.

'What *you're* thinking?' she said. 'Oh, I don't quite think we were finished with your amazing assessment of what *I* was offering. It was apparently "written all over me"—remember?'

He smiled. 'Good call. Now, where was I...? Ah, yes.'

And he cupped her jaw again, brushed his thumb over her bottom lip, tugging it.

'This mouth... These lips... They are quite clearly promising what you plan to do with them.'

'And that is...?'

He could hardly hear her. Was it the blood rushing in his ears or her sexy breathlessness—he had no idea. But he held her right where he wanted her, slid his hands further into her hair and positioned her at the slight angle he preferred. And then he waited. This was too divine to rush. She was easily the most tempting morsel he'd ever had—the last thing he was going to do was gorge on her out here, in full view of everyone.

But that didn't mean he couldn't have just a little taste.

He moved them together, so close only a sliver of air was between their mouths.

'You were saying…?' she whispered.

And as she spoke her lips brushed his and his resolve evaporated. He covered her mouth with his own in a hungry, passionate kiss and it was all he had known it would be. Soft, sweet and pure hot heaven.

Her lips were the perfect fit, the perfect pout. He made her deliver up kiss after kiss as he bit down on his resolve to keep them both decent. But with her breasts pressed fully against his body and his erection straining against her stomach it took all of his will to stay in a low gear.

'I was saying—before you interrupted—that these lips…' He slid his tongue over them. She whimpered. 'These lips have been telegraphing to me…'

He used his tongue to flick from the centre of her open pout to the upper edge of her top lip. And back. All the way along.

'That they're going to kiss every last part of me. Every. Part. Isn't that right, Princess?'

He felt her tongue dart out to meet his and the need to grind into her almost felled him. This game was overplayed. The public version, anyway. He grabbed her hand, looked up and down the jetty.

'We'll finish this back on the *Sea Devil*. Come on.'

He took her hand and almost marched her further along the runway to where a row of silently bobbing motorboats waited. He spotted his launch, stepped down and held out his hand, anxious to get this precious cargo aboard quickly.

His heart was hammering as he reached for her, and in one movement he'd tucked her close and taken his place behind the wheel. She leaned right in tight as he nosed the boat carefully around and out past the other launches. They came alongside the *Marengo*, its huge gleaming sides bearing down on them as he passed it and moved out into the bay.

In less than ten minutes he'd have her across the water, and five after that he'd have her across his bed.

The throb of the motor and the crash of the waves joined a crescendo of sensations with more to come. Dante loved this part of the chase—the anticipation, the build-up. The arc of tension gathering height until he could let his mind empty and his body just feel. And this felt *right*. This felt as if the particular symphony they were co-composing was going to have all the depth and drama he needed.

So she hated crowds...had social anxiety. So what? She was well in command of herself where her libido was concerned—that was for sure. And he could handle those emotions once they started to show.

But wasn't that the part that was dangerous? Wasn't that why you gave her the big brush-off earlier?

Like a mallet to a polo ball, he struck those thoughts out of his mind. He felt Lucie leaning against the crescent of his arm and shut out anything that was set to interrupt his mood. Wasn't that what he was best at?

No words passed between them as he cut the engine and tossed the speedboat's rope onto the yacht. He stepped out deftly, tied her up, and then held out his hand and guided her aboard the *Sea Devil*.

A third of the size of the *Marengo*, it was fast, sleek, and reflected the only aspect of his personality he was prepared to go public with—he gathered no moss. He was no apologist for liking things the way he liked them. Another benefit of the single life— no compromise in pretty much anything. Of course he'd had girlfriends who had tried to soften things up, the way women did, and that was fine. As far as it went. But it did no one any favours if you let them think they were going to gain permanency rights.

Permanency was the last thing he wanted to think about as he led Her Ladyship by the hand up the three steps to the sundeck. Darkness swathed the night, backlit by the pinpricks of deck lights. There was nobody else on board, his staff having taken him at his word and gone off for the weekend. Good for them—they worked hard. And good for him too, as it now turned out.

'I half expected there would be some party in full swing,' she said aloud, her cut-glass tones slicing through the night.

'*I'm* the party—remember?' he said as he moved them further along and down into a sunken area.

Plump banquettes skirted the space, and were scattered with an array of cushions—and that was as feminine as it got. A black glass table sat between three sides, and on the other side lay loungers in various positions. A small plunge pool to the left sank down even further, and more seats and beds were arranged there. It was comfortable. He liked it.

He switched on the side lights and quickly selected a muted melody underscored with the low throb of African drums. He poured them both champagne and walked to where Lucie had stalled in the middle of the space and was gently swaying her hips. He paused. Watched her.

She didn't ooze sexuality, the way some women did but, regarding her now, he saw that what she lacked in overt, in-your-face eroticism she more than made up for in sensuality—it ran through her like the bass line in the tune that was pulsing around them right now.

'Perfect…thank you,' she said as she took the glass from him and took a sip. Nervously?

'You know, I heard the staff call this boat "Dante's Lair" earlier today?'

Had she, indeed? He shrugged it off.

'People like to speculate, I suppose. They imagine they know all about me and my business.'

And they knew nothing. Why should they? His own parents had no idea of half the things he'd done. He wasn't the type to bleat about his woes. He and his brother, Rocco, had been brought up to be independent, to stand tall. The last thing he'd ever do was feel sorry for himself. Or, worse, let his guard down.

He had a great life. Gloss and glamour and good times. He knew how lucky he was—how much of a good start he'd had compared to his adopted brother. He'd never had to run in the streets to survive. He'd had everything he'd ever wanted. His mother hadn't been the most demonstrative with her affection, but he'd wanted for nothing. So when a bit of a trauma like Celine had come along he'd been able to deal with it. Of course he had. He hadn't told a living soul—hadn't needed to. He could handle life.

The Hermidas were proud—every last one of them. Proud and silent. And that was what made them so interesting to the press.

'"Lair" suggests something of a predator though.'

'Do you think that about me, Princess? That I'm predating on you? Right now?'

'Hardly,' she answered wryly, touching her hair. 'As far as I recall it was me that suggested this… this…'

He walked to her. 'This…private party?'

'Exactly,' she said, looking very much as if that

was the only type of party she would consider attending. The long swish of her blonde hair obscured one eye, starlet style, and she completed the look with another coy smile.

He almost shook his head at her. Who would believe this confident, in command woman was the same one who had literally begged him to help her out at the charity auction earlier.

'Maybe, but you must know that despite what's said about me I'm very choosy about who I allow into my…lair.'

He lifted the glass from her hand and set them both down on the table.

'I take it I am supposed to consider that a compliment?'

'All I'm saying is that being a princess doesn't give you any special rights.'

She smiled through the eyes she narrowed at him.

'You're not going to give up with that, are you?'

He winked slightly. 'I might. Depends…'

'On what, exactly?'

'On whether you're going to follow through with all those signals you've been telegraphing since the first moment I saw you.'

'Oh, that's right. Something about my filthy mind and my suggestive mouth. Was that it?'

The bubbling of the hot tub suddenly seemed to fill the night air. Dante nodded to it. Lucie's eyes drifted over, and then flipped right back to his.

'Not forgetting your body—which I recall was

a lot less covered up then. And. Completely. Soaking. Wet.'

She seemed to take that like a sucker punch, and her hand slid to her chest. Her mouth formed a silent 'oh' and for a second he thought he had genuinely shocked her. Then she slipped him another smile. Oh, yes, she was feeling it as much as he was.

'What are you suggesting, Dante?'

He started to unbutton his shirt. 'Princess, I'm well past the point of suggestion.'

The hand at her chest went to her mouth now. Oh, she was very, *very* good. Coy and cute and causing him all sorts of constriction issues. He tossed away his shirt and laid his hand on his belt, ran the leather through the loops and pulled it free. His erection strained uncomfortably as he tugged down the zip and yanked off his trousers.

Still she stood there, in her Little Miss Innocent pose. He had to laugh.

He gripped the sides of his boxers, raised his eyebrows and gave her a full-beam grin.

'Seems like we're right back where we started, Princess.'

She was still standing as if she'd been struck by lightning. Just as she had when he'd scared her off the boat earlier. Only this time the last thing he wanted her to do was disappear overboard.

But she didn't move a muscle and the glimmer of a red flag suddenly waved in his mind. Surely this was an act? Surely she wasn't *really* freaked out by his nudity?

'I hope you're not going to abandon ship this time?'

There was nothing else for it—he tugged down his boxers, releasing himself. Then he stood up and faced her head-on—fully hard, fully erect and fully loaded.

Lucie stood utterly still, but her eyes zoned straight in on him. Seconds ticked by as she gorged on the sight of him, and he felt so damn turned on that he put his hand around himself and stroked. This was getting out of hand before it had even begun.

'You'd better make your mind up, because soon I might not be in any fit state to rescue you.'

Another long beat as he continued to stroke, and she continued to stand, and then suddenly she began to walk towards him, her eyes trained directly on his. For some bizarre reason he felt as if he were guiding her across a rope bridge, willing her to take the next step. But that was just ridiculous.

'Nice to see you,' he said as she stepped into his space.

He placed his hands on either side of her jaw and closed the last inches between them. And then he pressed his lips to hers and kissed her.

Some kisses were sweet. Some kisses were hot.

Dante felt as if sunspots were bursting in front of his eyes and all through his body as his tongue slid into Lucie's warm, wet mouth and found hers.

He thought he could hear moans and sighs escaping her, but that might just as easily be him. Her lips and his lips and her face and his face had become one.

He grabbed her and plunged and plundered and savoured. His hands were in her hair, on her neck, her shoulders, her beautiful cleavage. He was unstoppable.

'Lucie, if you want to wear that dress ever again you'd better take it off now, before I rip—'

But the control he normally had in spades had evaporated before he could even finish the sentence and he spun her round and pulled.

Harnessed by her sleeves, she stood before him, her hair wild, her eyes wilder. Her mouth was wet and open and her breasts were almost completely bare. She looked more feral than regal, but he knew then that he had never seen a more beautiful woman in his life.

'Too late, I guess,' he said, reaching for her jaw and then latching his mouth onto the nipple he'd released from the veil of strained fabric.

She screamed, he thought, but it was as much as he could do not to throw her to the ground as he kept up the pressure on her nipple. Round and round he moved his tongue, sucking and tugging, and moulding with his other hand. Such full, beautiful breasts. He palmed and weighed and shaped them as he moved his mouth from one to the other, as each bud hardened to a point he knew would be bringing her intolerable, exquisite pleasure.

And, yes, he knew she was breathlessly begging him to stop, but that only drove him on. Until he felt her hands on his shoulders and realised he was bearing her weight. He straightened, scooped her up then spun her round and tugged the dress down further.

'This has got to go,' he said as he found the buttons that were hidden and ripped at them.

Her dress came apart in his hands. He looked at the shards of silk and then at the pale-skinned goddess before him. Her face was flushed and her breasts were soaked where his mouth had sucked and teased them. Her waist, flaring out to the perfect balance of feminine hips, was scored with tiny marks.

'Hey...' he said, smoothing his fingers over them. 'Sweetheart, was that me? Did I hurt you?'

She looked at him, and then down at herself, frowning for a brief moment. 'What?' she breathed. 'Hurt me...? No.'

He stepped up to her, his erection immediately pressing down against her stomach. He so badly needed to be deep inside her.

He lifted her. He couldn't stop himself. He placed himself neatly in between her legs. Immediately she hooked her legs round his waist and threw back her head.

A loud, low groan escaped from his mouth.

'Oh, yes, you're quite the princess for everyone else...but you're one very dirty girl for me.'

He glanced around—a wall, a floor, a sofa—he

had to lay her down somewhere. But nothing was right. She deserved better.

'Let's do this properly,' he said.

And he stepped past the hot tub, past the cushion-strewn banquettes and discarded scraps of fabric and clothes. And then he walked with her, naked but for the last scrap of silk and the teetering heels that pierced his flesh with each step. Down three stairs and on through the salon. Along the passageway that led to his suite. The lamps were low, sending soft Vs of light over the slices of dark polished wood that were used throughout the yacht. It wasn't cold—far from it—but Dante hugged her body close to his, protecting her.

Opening up the door of his suite, he saw the panoramic windows displaying a view of the whole of the bay. Of course the *Marengo*—stupendous—presided over the whole space, even at this distance. But she was the last thing Dante wanted to look at right now, and he quickly pressed the button that slid the curtains closed, closing off the twinkling night and any nosy paparazzi that might be circling like the sharks they were.

The *Sea Devil* might have already appeared on every piece of trashy, glossy paper and online feature, but Dante was always well aware of what was going to be published before it happened. *He* was in control of what the world saw. And he had a sixth sense that he really *didn't* want the world to have even a glimpse of this particular assignation. Oh, no. This was indeed a strictly private party.

He stepped fully into the room, feet landing on soft, plush carpet. The door closed behind them.

Immediately he felt her hands on his head, cupping his cheeks. She was kissing him deeply, passionately, and with a wantonness he was finding harder and harder to resist.

Blindly he stepped forward, past the four club chairs and the walnut coffee table, his thigh dragging against the skirt of one of the cabinets that arced from one end of the room to the other.

The bed.

He felt his leg bump against it and grabbed Lucie's wrists, pulling them back from his head and her mouth from his face. He held her and looked at her make-up-smudged eyes and hot pink cheeks.

'You beautiful girl,' he said.

And he set her down on his bed.

She blinked at him as she kneeled up, and for a moment a sad little smile graced her face. 'Well, we both know that's stretching it a bit, Dante. Nice of you, though.'

He frowned at her. What on earth was going through her mind?

'Sweetheart, you're beautiful—believe me.'

'Anyone can be beautiful with a stylist and a bucket of make-up. I hardly think I still qualify all these hours later.'

She had no idea.

'I'm no fantasist—I know my limitations.'

'Is that a fact?' he said, bending towards her and letting his breath seep in through the fine silk of her panties. 'Why don't you lie back here and I'll show you how lovely you are.'

And he kneeled before her and put his hands on her hips, then round to the curve of her bottom, moulding and kneading, urging her legs a little more open.

'Dante, please!' she said.

'I want to kiss you here,' he said, ignoring her gasp as he bent to press a kiss between her legs. 'Take these off.'

With one hand he held her by the waist and with the other he tugged down her panties, again feeling that growing realisation that she was...*shy*?

But he knew women, and he knew what they loved.

She lay back now, as he gripped her ankles and tugged her legs open, ignoring her little squeal. She was outstanding. Completely. Never shifting his gaze, he took a single finger and gently stroked his way slowly between the swollen lips, slicking the wet flesh until he came upon the tiny hard nub. With a harder rub he pressed, until he heard her cry out in pleasure.

He placed one hand on each of her thighs and started to dip his head forward. There was nothing he wanted to do more than feel his mouth at her core, taste her. He tried to hook her legs over his shoulders, but as he looked up at her lush body, saw her eyes wide and watchful, suddenly she jerked up and slipped out from under him.

He made another deep, throaty sound and then he dipped his head. He so badly wanted to lap her with his tongue.

'Dante, please. I really don't want you to do that.'

'Honey, you'll love it,' he said, barely pausing.

'No, honestly,' she said, struggling away from him. He stopped. Instantly. Leaned up. Backed off.

'Hey, if you're not comfortable this stops now.'

There was no way on this earth he would ever force himself on a woman, no matter how his sanity depended on it. But this one was outdoing herself with the conflicting signals.

Sudden silence fell between them. He waited a moment, then made to stand up. He'd known this was a bad idea. She was a whole bag full of issues—and none of them easy to solve.

'Time out,' he said.

'Please, don't— I really want to— I want you…'
She reached for him—lunged.

'I'm sorry. I want you so much. Please, Dante.'

And she kneeled up, wound her arms around his neck and slid her beautiful lush body against him.

He took her wrists, held her back even as his body reacted.

'We're mature adults. Mature, *consenting* adults. This is not about coercion. Ever.'

'I know,' she breathed, staring up with big bruised eyes. She was all vixen again. God, she killed him.

But there was no way he was going to do anything with a woman who wasn't as into it as he.

'Dante, there is nothing I want to do more right now than this.'

She held his eye, then leaned forward to cup his face. His eyes fell to her full breasts, swinging towards him. Still he held back. Until her tongue eased his lips apart and slid into his mouth. He felt the very tips of her nipples graze his chest. And then the rest of her.

She pulled him down as she lay back and he let her. He let go. Her legs slid round his back. He was big, and he really didn't want to hurt her, but when he stalled after only an inch the need to fill her battled with the need to answer the nagging doubt that was creeping into his head again.

'Please don't stop,' she breathed, tightening her legs and tilting her hips.

She reached her arms up and pulled him down into a kiss he could no more resist than resist taking his next breath. She defined *irresistible*.

He tried again. So sweet and so tight...but something was just not right.

Her eyes, when she opened them to see why he had stopped, were anxious.

'Lucie, are you sure you've done this before?' he asked, not even knowing himself that those words had been going to come out of his mouth. It seemed ridiculous—but he had to know...

She glanced away.

'Sweetheart?'

'I never said I had or I hadn't—but I want to—so badly. Please, Dante.'

He looked bewildered. 'Are you telling me you're a *virgin*?'

He shook his head at his own stupidity. She was so adamant. So resolute. And she just *did* it for him. Completely.

When she didn't answer he rolled that around in his mind for a bewildered second even as she moved under him, used the legs hooked round his back to pull him nearer. He groaned as he felt himself slide in deeper. And then deeper still. And then he could only follow the urges of his body until he was buried in her to the hilt.

'Oh, angel, you're killing me.'

She moaned, deep and long, and he'd never felt such a perfect fit—it was visceral. He bent down and kissed her, drinking in the sounds of her satisfaction and starting to pulse to the tempo of his own.

'You feel amazing,' she whispered against his neck.

She whispered his name. He whispered hers back, asked her if she was okay. Because *he* was. More than okay. And the sensation of being inside her, so hot and deep and primal, was absolutely right. That was it—he felt absolutely *right*.

He looked down at her—at her face, her breasts, where he was sliding in and out. Then back to her face. She was with him all the way. And then she began to cry with her own pleasure and he knew he was stroking that special place.

'You're okay?'

She opened eyes that had been closed and smiled at him. She didn't look remotely virginal.

'Oh, yes. Never better.'

'Oh, I think we can do better.'

And he tilted her hips up higher and drove in deeper. He felt his climax coming like a freight train—unstoppable and thunderous—and he called his release out to the night, unguarded and unedited.

Dante rolled to one side and lay on his back, his arms above his head. He could feel Lucie turning onto her side and moving to close the distance between them.

Had that really just happened?

The best sex of his life with a…?

He couldn't get this straight in his head. Had to process it. He sat on the edge of the bed, heard her shift behind him. Then the heavy fog of silence.

'Was that your first time?'

He tilted his head—didn't look but waited to hear the truth.

Nothing. Except the wispy strains of music that emanated from the salon and the unravelling of the moments they had just shared. Then her hand…burning on his back—only her fingertips, but still he felt as if he had been scalded and jerked away.

He stood up. 'I'm going to hit the shower.'

He should have listened to his gut. Should have let his eyes see the red flag that had fluttered in the corner of his mind. Should have stopped when he'd first had that inkling. What an idiot! Lose himself in a woman? An evening of no-strings sex? With English aristocracy who turned out to be a virgin. A virgin who had decided to relinquish that status with *him*. Tonight. *Now.*

You couldn't make this stuff up.

He turned on the shower and stepped in, caught a glimpse of himself in the mirror as the steam crept across it like an embarrassed flush. He looked haunted—grim. His eyes had been dulled by the effort of holding it together and then letting it all out in—*that woman.*

What a woman.

Damn her. What on earth had just happened? *Why* him? Why *now*? Women were such devious, scheming creatures. There was *always* an ulterior motive. Every time!

He racked his brains, trying to think of what she might hope to get out of it, what emotional ransom she was going to hold him to. She didn't need money, she certainly didn't need fame. He didn't think she'd been bluffing when she'd told him of her shyness. And she was so beautiful she could have her pick of men.

Yet she'd waited until tonight to have sex.

With a man she'd made no secret of hating from the first moment they'd met…

Was it payback for something he'd done? It was the best payback he could imagine if that was the case!

It was incomprehensible—but when it came to women nothing would surprise him. Who knew what was going on in those pretty little heads? Those months with Celine had taught him that, at least. She had been a woman who would stop at nothing to get what she wanted. The carefully executed seduction... the lies and then the venom... And then the final act.

Dante felt the water streaming down his face. He rubbed the back of his neck with both hands and shook his head.

Images of Celine—or Miss di Rosso, as she'd been then—seeped into his brain. The first time he'd seen her, in that tight, bright skirt, walking through a vale of sunbeams in the cloisters with the school principal. He'd fallen in love with her then—everyone had. The only sexy young female teacher in a boys' boarding school. It had been inevitable that she would become the pin-up girl.

But of all the men and boys there she'd targeted *him*—leaning over him, her blouse artfully undone, while he sat powerless with an erection under his desk. Then the 'extra lessons' she'd felt he should have. Slowly, carefully, she had seduced him into a secret world. A world where he'd felt like a king compared to his classmates. He was screwing the object of their wet dreams and she was screwing his mind.

He'd felt like that right up until the moment when it had all become so obvious. When the lust he'd been feeling hadn't turned into the love she'd demanded. That was when he'd drawn back. Right at that moment. And then the tables had turned. Spectacularly.

But that had been fifteen years ago. And he'd been on his guard ever since. Nothing had got past his impenetrable shield. No one could see through the smiling, charming, engaging young man he'd become since those dark months.

Dante squeezed some shower gel onto his hand and the lemon scent of it burst through his senses— just as the image of Lucie's trusting eyes burst into his mind. He frowned at the memory of that moment. It had felt as if he'd—*let her in*. There was no other way of saying it.

Well, that was definitely not going to happen again.

Lucie could hardly bear to look at the perfect picture of his backside, walking away. She drew her eyes quickly to the small slice of window that was not covered over by curtains. It was still terribly dark outside. The faintest trace of lilac laced the horizon but it would be hours until sunrise. Her strappy shoes lay on the pearl carpet. Her dress was back in that salon. Lying like a puddle of satin where he had as good as ripped it off.

So *that* was what it was all about.

She squeezed her eyes shut and let the feelings flow over her again. She'd never have believed anyone could make her feel like that. It had been beyond fantastic. *Way* beyond. Her body was liquid, melting after his touch. And she'd almost, *almost* let him kiss between her legs.

Almost—but, no, she couldn't. Not *there*. She didn't want to think about it.

She opened her eyes and stared at the wall. The shower was running, the sound muted through the veneer walls of the bedroom. She lay back and stared up at the ceiling. What should she do? Leave? Join him in the shower? Lie here and wait for the second course? Was this normal behaviour for a man? If so it was terribly disappointing.

She sighed and shook her head. She certainly wasn't going to wait around to find out.

She wrapped herself up in a sheet and went over to the panoramic window. Framed there, between the slightly open curtains, was the bay. The *Marengo* was in pride of place at the jetty. Lights still twinkled, but the great big thing was always lit up—in perpetual readiness for the next port, the next party, which her father had let slip was to be in Florida.

The crew had two weeks to sail her there. She had planned on staying on overnight and then heading back to the villa later today. Now she was stuck on the other side of the dratted bay, and she'd be damned if she was going to swim back a second time.

The door of the en-suite bathroom opened.

She saw his reflection in the window. A puff of steam and then the man himself, in a shaft of light, a black towel wrapped around his hips. He glanced at her. Just for a second. Then he moved across his room, every step emphasising that this was *his* place. His *lair*.

'You're welcome to use the shower,' he said.

She processed his tone. She was good at that, having learned from a very early age to work out which of her mother's moods was in operation at any given time. That had helped her to modify her own responses and behaviour, to work out when to melt into the background—which had almost always been the best thing to do.

This tone from Dante…?

She barely knew him, but one thing she'd picked up was that there was a storm behind all that sunshine. He could turn it on and off. On and off. Stepping up to take charge of the auction he'd been at his sunniest. Standing like a statue in the middle of the dance floor he'd been at his most thunderous. He'd looked then as if he'd like to rip someone's head off. And then he'd slipped back into laconic, lazy lover mode. But there was something dark, something lurking behind that dimpled grin and sexy walk. She could feel it.

But that was no reason to be so hideously inconsiderate. None.

'Thank you,' she said, 'but I'd rather get going.'

He pulled the towel off. Uninhibited. Totally. Dried himself and then tossed it onto the bed.

'Look. If I'm angry with you it's because you didn't tell me about your sexual past—or lack of one.'

Lucie was stunned. That was the last thing she'd expected to hear. He couldn't possibly be bothered about her inexperience. Deflowering virgins was something that men boasted about. Stupid men, admittedly.

'Well, gosh, I'm sorry. If I'd known it was such a big deal I would have had a T-shirt made.'

He was walking to one of the cherrywood cabinets when he stopped and cast her a look down the side of his face.

'Sarcasm doesn't suit you, Lucie.'

'No more than contempt suits *you*.'

'If that's how you interpret it, then I'm sorry. But I'm serious—you should have told me about being a virgin.'

'You would have stopped.'

He started moving again. Reached into a drawer and pulled on a pair of super-tight, super-sexy black boxers. She tried so hard not to stare—but how on earth did he expect her to keep the drool in her mouth when he was standing in front of her looking as if he'd just stepped from the pages of a magazine?

'I would have stopped for good reason, Lucie.' He straightened and then reached into another drawer. He pulled out a T-shirt and slid it over his head. The shock of damp blond hair fell into place perfectly.

'You're not a silly little girl—you're a mature woman. And you've chosen to sleep with your first ever sexual partner *tonight*? What am I supposed to think? It was clearly important for you to keep yourself chaste all these years—how old are you, anyway?'

He was frowning. There was no trace whatsoever of Mr Sunshine.

'I am twenty-five, since you ask. So charmingly.'

She sounded awful, she knew—like some kind of snobbish harpy. And she was beginning to see his point of view. But for heaven's sake...

'My point exactly. *Twenty-five-year-old princess beds Argentinian polo player in Get Rid of Virginity Quick game.* Yeah? See how those headlines would read? Some people might say you used me.'

'I did not use you!'

He was now pulling on a pair of jeans, sliding a belt through the loops and buckling it. He eyed her sceptically.

'Don't be ridiculous,' she said, puffing herself up as much as she could while draped in a sheet. 'Everyone knows that women don't have equal rights in the bedroom. Men are sexual predators who take what they want, and the more that they do, the more they're admired. What a stud! What a hero! The minute a woman goes after what she wants she's a tart.'

Suddenly the storm broke. Thunder spread across his brow.

'You think so? You think that's *always* how it works? Well, take it from me: there are a lot more female predators out there than you might imagine.'

He blasted out the words. Fury laced every syllable. It was like being in the eye of a typhoon that had come right out of nowhere. She stood, stunned, waiting to be sure that the storm had passed before she spoke.

'And your actions tonight could be interpreted as predatory...'

Now he was barely audible, moving about, running his hands through his hair, avoiding any eye contact.

'Even *you* don't believe that I'm a sexual predator! How ridiculous! Listen to yourself. You know perfectly well that all that happened was that we were both in the right place at the right time. You wanted it as much as I did.'

'You really expect me to believe that it was just a question of "tonight's the night"? After twenty-five years?'

'Look, I don't expect you to believe anything.'

'But you still owe me an explanation.'

He kept his back to her, sat on the edge of the bed pulling on deck shoes.

'How about this, then? Yes, I used you. I used you for sex. But you can be sure there won't be a repeat of it.' She sounded shrill. She sounded waspish.

He stood up. Faced her. Hands on hips. Raised eyebrows.

'Yeah, well, that was always a cert.'

Lucie stared. 'You really are just another insensitive pig.'

And she walked in the column of her sheet, with as much grace as she could muster, to the door. She heaved it open and made her way back along the corridor. She passed the hot tub, bubbling away under dawn's canopy, and stepped up into the salon, spotting her dress immediately in its shards of shame. She grabbed up her underwear and tried to wriggle into it.

How the heck was she going to get ashore? She'd rather die than ask him for a lift in the speedboat. Could she swim? Call a water taxi?

She was desperately fastening the legions of buttons when she heard him come close. Suddenly protecting her own space became the most critical thing she could do. She dropped the dress and gathered up the sheet.

'Even an insensitive pig like me knows a liar when he sees one.'

She turned to face him. He was leaning casually, one arm on the doorframe, head cocked to one side—but he looked as relaxed as a starched shirt.

'What's that supposed to mean?'

'You really need me to spell it out? Okay. I've known you less than twenty-four hours. But in that time I think I've seen every one of your princess-cut diamond faces. You went from the rudest, most ungrateful bitch I've ever met to a—a wreck.'

Lucie stood her ground as he straightened up and began to pace towards her.

'That panic attack? It nearly drew the curtains

on your big night. And it was the only reason you even gave me entry to your father's yacht. If I hadn't stepped up you would have had me clapped in irons and thrown in the—the tower, or whatever you aristocrats do. And then something happened. Because the next thing I know you're hunting me down and offering yourself to me on a plate.'

He paused and stared at her with that penetrating gaze. She was determined to hold his eye—to stare right back while she fired a retort. But it was useless. He was right. She *had* used him. And she'd lied to him. How awful. How utterly, disgracefully awful.

She stepped away, bowed her head.

'When I rescued you the last thing you had on your mind was losing your virginity. Isn't that right?' he asked.

She opened her mouth but he put up his hand to stop her.

'Yes, I *know* you didn't need to be rescued. And I know that I probably upset the whole of the marine biodiversity of the Caribbean—but that's not the point. Here,' he said, holding out her shoes. 'Tell me I'm wrong.'

Lucie reached for her shoes but he held them just out of reach and eyed her carefully. Through the haze of guilt she cast him a quick look and grabbed for them again. This time he shook his head and released them.

She clutched them and moved away.

'Lucie?'

'Yes—okay,' she said. 'I hated you from the minute I saw you.' She turned round to face him. 'And when you came on the yacht I hated you even more.'

She had. All that arrogance. While she'd been feeling so wretched! Thinking he might be her *mother*, of all people.

Her mother—who had let her down. Who didn't have time to fulfil her promise but had all the time in the world to order Lucie about, demand that she do this or that. To tell her to stay away from the very person who had stepped up and actually helped her.

She turned to him. 'But I was genuinely grateful for what you did. You did more for me than anyone has ever done before—helping me out like that.'

He looked at her curiously. Suddenly she felt she'd gone too far. Given too much away. She tossed her head back.

'I wanted to taste forbidden fruit, if you like. I didn't intend that we would go as far as we did. I didn't think for a minute that I would sleep with you. But then I thought, *Why not?* That's all. There's no big mystery.'

She knew she sounded self-righteous. But wasn't that always the way?

She started furiously to pull the dress on. It was ripped at the shoulders and it was still a monster to get on, sticking at her hips and causing her to heave at it in an ungainly way. Her hands fumbled with the dratted buttons, missing the silk loops over and over, and suddenly it was too much.

Fiery tears formed in her eyes. She'd held herself together all night and now some stupid buttons were going to be her undoing? No way. *No.* She tried again. Bent her head and tried to manoeuvre her fingers while he stood utterly silent behind her. Damn him. *Damn.*

'You wait twenty-five years and then you think, *Why not?* I've had better compliments in my life.'

Her mind flashed with images of him worshipping her, mounting her, leaning down on her, glorying in her femininity and making her feel proud of her body for the first time she could remember.

'I'm sure you have.'

'So I was right the first time. You used me. I was just some kind of problem-solver—first with the auction and then with the virginity.'

How horrid. How utterly cold and calculating. Was that what he really thought of her? She could barely see her fingers through the thick, wobbling veil of unspilled tears in her eyes.

'If that's how you want to put it.' Her voice was choked and thin but she wouldn't turn her head, wouldn't let a single tear fall as the buttons—finally done—held the two torn sides of her dress together.

'I can't think of a better way.'

The hot tub bubbled back into life. Like some Greek chorus filling in every awkward pause.

'And the reason you had to lose your virginity tonight was…? Because, believe me, this is the part that really interests me.'

He really had her like a worm on a stick, turning it and making her squirm.

'Because of my mother,' she blurted, shocking herself with the words that had actually poured from her mouth.

'Your *mother*?'

Saying more would make her sound absolutely ridiculous. Saying less would be crazy. 'Yes. My mother has warned me my whole life to stay away from men like my father. Men like you.'

'Like me? You think I am like your father?'

'Yes—and when she found out you had replaced her at the auction she was furious.'

He narrowed one eye. 'Your mother was furious because she thinks I am like your father and that I replaced her. And *that's* why you slept with me?'

Lucie sat down heavily on a sofa and tried to stuff her toes under the narrow straps across her evening shoes.

'My mother is a bitch. That's why I slept with you.'

'Oh, that makes *so* much more sense.'

Lucie looked around for some kind of distraction. Her shoes were tied, her dress was on—she needed something to occupy her hands. There was nothing—except this great hunk of man in front of her, demanding answers.

'Okay. You really want to know? My mother was supposed to do this whole event with me. It's why the CCC approached me in the first place. I might raise two quid on my own, but Lady Viv could easily raise two million. I asked her. She knows how bad my social anxiety is, and she promised she would do it. I would never in a million years have got involved in any of this if she hadn't agreed. She said she would do it if I accepted her conditions— Oh, good grief. I don't even know why I'm telling you any of this.'

Suddenly his hands were round her upper arms, warm and steady. And his eyes were trained on hers.

'What conditions?'

Lucie pulled away—but he strengthened his grip.

'What conditions?'

'Look, none of that matters. She wants me to be more like her—and I'm nothing like her—and she doesn't care for the things I care for. That's all.'

'Like turtles?'

She turned on him.

'Hey! I'm serious—I'm not mocking! But you said "conditions". What conditions?'

How did she explain?

'Lose weight. Other things too, but mostly the weight.'

She couldn't look at him. Saying the words out loud made her feel ashamed.

She heard two things then—the beginning of a long whistle and the ringing pulse of a phone. She looked round for hers, then remembered she didn't have so much as a pocket handkerchief with her— and that her phone was drowning in an ice bucket somewhere.

Lucie followed Dante's gaze to where a phone was lighting up.

'It's fine. It's my mother. No one else would phone this early.'

Its ringing filled the air.

'Aren't you going to get it?'

He half-smiled, shook his head. 'No, I'm going to listen to the end of your story.'

'My story?'

He nodded his head. 'Everyone has their story. And it sounds like yours is quite a complicated one.'

'I'm really not in the habit of telling people my "story" or anything about me. So let's leave it at that.'

'Fine—except that your story now involves me. And it will for ever.'

She felt that stick poke her a little more keenly, and the worm squirmed a little more painfully. Normally when people got this interested she had no difficulty whatsoever in putting them in their place—or exiting. It was part of who she was—her essence. Nobody must know anything—ever.

And, yes, although that came more from her father than her mother, even Lady Viv 'managed' things. She only put out what she wanted. And she certainly wouldn't want anything like this. Wash dirty linen in public? *Never.* Though wasn't that exactly what she'd done to Lucie last night? She didn't care one iota about Lucie's public image, or rather public humiliation.

Yes, she had totally stepped over the line yesterday. Leaped over it. Way over.

'My mother courts attention. Craves attention. Needs it. I abhor it. She likes to look pretty. I don't. Look pretty. So I don't try.'

'Yes, you said that already. I have to say I'm not sure where all that ugly duckling delusion comes from.'

'Dante…' She sighed, almost exasperated. 'I'm what you'd call "the outdoors type". In England that means I'm at home in muddy fields—well, you have horses…you know what I mean. And over here it means that I swim, I tag animals, I run on the beach. I like what I like. And I don't try to be anyone else or please anyone else.'

'That's obvious.'

'Lady Viv is all about things being pretty.'

'And she finds it hard to accept that you're more than just pretty? You have depth.'

Lucie's eyes widened.

'And she's jealous of you.'

At that she laughed out loud. 'Don't be ridiculous. She's not jealous! She's *embarrassed* by me!'

The words hung in the air. Unsaid for all these years. Yet there they were—bold and ugly. But resonating with truth.

'I doubt that.'

'Do you?'

Lucie turned away from his gaze. It was too humiliating. She realised she must sound as if she wanted reassurance.

'Look, I don't care. I don't need anyone to tell

me what I've spent my life witnessing. It's fine. It is what it is.'

'You've really no idea.' He seemed to say it almost to himself. 'I really *do* have to spell it out to you.'

'No, you really don't. Trust me—the last thing I want is anyone's pity.'

'The last thing I'd *give* you is pity. But it seems to me that you're living under some grave misapprehensions. Anyway...' He smiled and rubbed his hands up and down her arms. 'You used me. For sex. The least you can do is indulge me.'

'Indulge you in what?'

Why did the smile that slid across his handsome face make her feel so warm and woozy? It was just a smile...a parting of the lips. Okay, his eyes crinkled and twinkled, but so what if the teeth he flashed were heart-stoppingly perfect? And, oh, those dimples—it was like being shot at close range, she would imagine, hit with both barrels.

His hands cupped her jaw. He pulled her closer.

'You are beautiful. You are sexy. And you care. Not just about what you're wearing. You care about important things. And you'll fight for them. Even if it means putting yourself out there.'

He kissed her, and she felt that something open and deep and raw was suddenly a little more exposed. And it frightened her. Who did he think he was, analysing her? She pulled away.

'That's very kind of you, but let's not start making stuff up to gild this particular lily. As I said, I really don't need it.'

'No—you need this.'

And as quickly as she'd pulled out of his grasp he'd pulled her back, turned her round and kissed her. Hard. And deep. And long.

She could fight or she could go with the flow. But after a single moment she knew that there was no real choice. A sigh as wild as the ocean breeze slid from mouth as she realised she could do nothing but answer his demands. He paced backwards, kissing her all the while, his mouth mastering her, his body hard and uncompromising and exactly what she'd never even known she needed.

'Don't you, Princess?'

He didn't wait for a reply. He slid his hand over her breast and then hoisted up her skirt. She groaned into his mouth.

'Payback begins now.'

With frenzied hands they ripped at each other's clothes. Her mouth covered every inch of his body, greedily grabbing and kissing and licking, and then she was lying down on one of the banquettes, and he was inside her, thrusting with all his might as he brought her with him to the very edge of passion and beyond.

This time when he rolled over she rolled with him. Her head lay on his chest and he wrapped her in his arms. Neither spoke. Through the windows the lilac dawn turned pink and then blue and the day awoke properly.

'What time do you think it is?' she asked, drawing patterns over his smooth bronze skin, marvelling at his male beauty.

When he didn't answer she cocked her head to look at him. He was staring straight up, unseeing.

'Oh, I'd say about ten. Listen, I've been thinking...'

At that the pulsing beat of his phone sounded again.

Dante loosened his arm from under her and reached over.

'Yep, right on cue,' he said, looking at the screen before pressing the button to answer.

'Good morning, Mother. It's still early. Though not as early as your last call.'

Lucie lay still, acutely aware of her nakedness and of the low burr of the woman's voice on the other end of the phone.

'Yes, of course—go right ahead. I haven't forgotten. I know how important this is for you—for all of us.'

He sat up, skilfully tucking two pillows behind him in a way that suggested he'd done it a thousand times before. A sharp sense of sadness suddenly struck her as she realised that, yes, he probably had—with a thousand different women in his bed.

So she had made a wonderful grand gesture to her mother, had she? She had *shown* her! Proved that she wasn't her property—that she had a mind of her own.

Really?

Maybe all she'd done was prove that she was another statistic.

'Yes, I was just about to sort it.'

She saw his fingers drum on the sheet as he shot her a quick glance. No, she mustn't think like that—she mustn't let all that mental chatter take her down the wrong path. She must think positively. She'd made a choice—she hadn't just thrown herself at the first man available. She had decided to step out of her mother's shade and into the light. *Dante's* light. And she felt warmed by it—not ashamed.

'Not at all, Mother.'

Lucie rolled round, pulled the sheet up to her chin and stared at the utterly perfect blue sky. Her mother would have made at least a dozen calls to Lucie's drowned phone by now. The last time Lucie had been incommunicado it had almost led to the armed guard being called. Leaving one's phone behind was the ultimate offence.

Calling was her mother's way of salving her conscience. She couldn't really care less what Lucie was up to, but she liked to be able to say with some certainty exactly where she was. And of course Lucie's role, as far as her mother was concerned, was to talk her back from the ledge when her own anxiety levels soared.

Like in the early days of her parents' separation,

when her father had been entertaining new lady-friends and Lucie had been expected to file a daily report to her inconsolable mother. Yes, she was always expected to be available—so goodness knew what kind of reception waited for her when Lady Viv finally did track her down.

'As soon as I know for sure I'll tell you.'

On the other hand maybe she *had* been a bit rash to throw her phone away like that. Her mother might actually be *worried* about her. It would be the first time, but then she'd never given her cause for concern before. Apart from that time when she'd sat on her phone and smashed the screen... Oh! Who could forget the barrage of abuse she'd faced for that?

If she hadn't let her bottom spread with all that horse-riding... If she'd been a bit more like Lady Viv in her day...

Lucie cringed, recalling that moment. She'd heard Badass and Simon laughing in the background after her mother's, 'You *sat* on it?' had been repeated three times with increasing volume.

'Today. Sure.' Dante whistled.

She really didn't want to be listening to his private call with his mother. She knew more than most how they could turn out. No—it was time to get off the boat, get back, and get on with the aftermath.

She sat up and reached for a second time for her clothes. The dress—minus another dozen or so buttons—lay at her feet, but she really had no other option and so began the arduous task of fastening it up again.

'Yes, you *know* I will.'

Something about his tone made Lucie pause. She was trying to fasten the stupid ankle straps on her shoes, but why bother? She could just as easily leave them hanging out of their ridiculous diamante loops.

'Give me five minutes. I'll call you right back.'

Maybe she should be giving him privacy, she thought, standing up and catching sight of herself in the mirror. How utterly ridiculous she looked. While Dante, also now standing up, walking around the bed, the purest, most male, handsomest form imaginable, was even more attractive than he looked with his clothes on. How was that possible?

He was walking round to her.

'Sorry about that—I had to take it.'

He hooked the phone against his neck as he smoothed one of the most engaging smiles she had ever seen all over his face. A double dimple. *Wow.*

'Lucie, what are your plans for the day?'

She mentally groaned at the thought of all those people crawling over the yacht, dismantling the party paraphernalia, wanting to ask her questions, getting into her space. She really ought to be there—she really oughtn't to have left. But she had and—damn it all—it had been so worth it.

'And the weekend?'

Well, that was easy—she would be fielding calls from her mother. There would be, *Where the hell have you been?* and then, *Who the hell were you with?* and undoubtedly, *Have I taught you nothing?* Then some sort of symbolic wringing of the hands, and after about ten seconds it would be all about Lady Viv again.

Only if she let it, she reminded herself. She'd had a lovely evening, and the last thing she was going to do was let her mother spoil it by dissecting it. There were some things at least that she could keep private.

'Only, if you've no particular plans I'd like you to come up to New York with me.'

He was moving about in that easy Hollywood way he had, as if the cameras were rolling, the director was in his chair and she was the starlet waiting to speak her lines. She narrowed her eyes.

'New York?'

He nodded.

'My mother is due to collect an award at the Woman of the Year Awards next weekend. There has been a lot of speculation in the press about it—I don't know if you keep up with all that stuff? Anyway, we've all got to put on a show for Eleanor, and I need to take a date. Princess, I can't think of anyone who would slip into the role better than you.'

She turned. She faced him. She could see herself in the mirror, with last night smeared all over her. And he'd just asked her out on a date? To an awards ceremony? With the rest of the Hermida family and the whole world watching?

'It's very flattering, but I don't know if that is such a great idea.'

'Why wouldn't it be a great idea?'

Lucie tried not to look at her reflection. 'Well, it would be public, I assume? If the press are all over it before it's actually happened, they're going to be even more interested when it does.'

She thought she heard him draw in a breath.

'And the problem with it being public is…?'

Cameras. Photographers. Lady Vivienne Bond, she thought, wincing.

'It's just not my thing. You know that.'

'I know that I'd like you to come with me.'

'But there must be tons of girls who could go with you. Girls who would actually *enjoy* getting all dressed up in—' she held out the skirts of the satin dress '—one of these.'

He laughed. 'It's not exactly torture, is it?'

She scowled, saw that blasted reflection again. 'Look, it's not my thing. And my mother would—'

'Ah, that's it, isn't it? Your mother would…?'

He held her gaze—worse, he *probed* her gaze. She felt as if he were looking right inside her mind. She glanced away.

'What would your mother do, Lucie? Disapprove? Are the aristocracy only supposed to date other aristocrats? Is that it?' He took a step towards her, laughed. 'Am I too low-rent for you, Princess?'

'Oh, stop it! You know I was only kidding.'

'Were you? Look, I don't give a damn what your

mother or anyone else thinks—I need a date for this event, that's all. Someone who—*gets* it.'

'Gets what?'

'That it's just a date. A no-strings-attached, short-term, all-you-can-eat buffet, and then—goodbye.'

'Sounds…filling.'

He laughed. 'You see—you get it. Plus, you know what cutlery to use. I don't need to worry that you'll use your fish knife to spread butter on your napkin, or any other crime of the century like that.'

'It's not exactly a hanging offence.'

'Well, not to me and you—but to someone like my mother it's on a par with genocide. *"There are certain standards, Dante, and you know what they are…"'*

The low, slow tones he used to mimic Eleanor Hermida made her instantly compare them to Lady Viv's shrill staccato.

'And, for all I normally don't give a damn about melon forks and steak knives, this is her special day, and it would be *very* nice…' his cheeks slid into two slight furrows and his eyes twinkled endearingly '… if you would come along and show us all how it's done. It's not you who'll be in the spotlight. It's my mother. You'll just be there to make up the numbers.'

'Gosh, you make it sound so tempting.'

'Plus you get to seriously annoy your mother. Put another bit of emotional distance between you.'

'We're as emotionally distant as the two poles as it is. But I like your logic.'

'So we have a deal?'

'Let me go over this again. I come as your date on an all-inclusive, no-strings weekend and then we never meet again? And I do this because it will annoy my mother? It sounds childish.'

'It sounds perfect. It demonstrates much more effectively than words that you are your own boss. That you make your own choices and are answerable to yourself. And it has the advantage of being very public. There's no mistaking your intention.'

'And the no-strings bit?'

He looked at her sharply. 'That is non-negotiable.'

'Absolutely! As long as we're both clear.'

It was all very well to use a weekend with Dante to drive a long overdue wedge between herself and her mother. But there was no way she wanted to end up like her. Worrying over a playboy. Good grief, no!

'Crystal,' he said.

She stood in last night's rags, with last night's make-up gone and her hair flat and fallen. But this time when she looked at herself in the mirror she saw tomorrow's woman. Something had happened overnight. Whatever her motivation—and she wasn't *entirely* blind to the fact that of all the men in all the world she'd chosen the handsomest one to spend her first ever night with, and she wasn't *entirely* deaf to the little alarm bell that had rung at 'no strings'— she had taken a major step down a brand-new path. And she had liked it.

'So I come to New York…? What are the rest of the details?'

'We fly first to the Hamptons. There's a business deal I'm considering there. I've been putting it off, but I need to make a decision before I head to Dubai.'

He spoke quietly, gravely, and she saw then that there was more—much more—to him than a polo-playing playboy.

'Yes. We'll go there, hang out for a couple of days, see some friends, and I'll get this tied up. Then New York. With the family. But that's it. No, *Wouldn't it be nice if…?*—none of that. It's these few days and then we split.'

As if she needed any clearer explanation, he lifted his arms and pointed with each finger in the opposite direction.

'Look, I'm perfectly clear on that—you don't need to worry. And, sorry if this comes as a shock, I have no intention whatsoever of pursuing a romance with you. You're really not my type.'

'Pardon me?'

Lucie couldn't stifle a smirk.

'What? Hasn't anyone ever told you that before? You look as if I've just delivered the news that you've got two heads. Sorry, Dante, but you're not my type. It's that simple.'

He swiftly gathered himself together again, but there was no mistaking that it looked as if this was the first time in his life he'd ever been told *Thanks, but no thanks* by a woman. It certainly wouldn't do him any harm.

'What's not "your type" about what we just did? I don't recall you telling me that you'd had better.'

'I don't recall telling you that I'd had *anything*! There was no one before to compare you to.'

He was now pulling on jeans, fastening buttons, looking as if he had not a care in the world more than what shade of T-shirt he might choose. But she could taste a lick of tension in the air and see the edge of strain across his brow.

'Sorry—that came out all wrong. What I mean is—what I *mean* is that I've been surrounded by playboys my whole life. My own father practically invented the word! I've seen at very close range the devastation that they bring. So, lovely as you are, the last thing on this earth I want to be is anywhere near you after this weekend.'

Grey T-shirt selected and pulled down over his perfect golden torso, hair flicked effortlessly back into place and beautiful one-dimple smile slipped on, Dante faced her.

'Well, I'm glad we've got that cleared up. I'd hate to think that those screaming orgasms you had were such a disappointment.'

Lucie smiled through the flush of shame that she felt creep warmly over her chest and neck. Would she ever be able to think again of those moments without feeling a stab, a shadow, an echo of how he'd made

her feel? But there was no way she was letting him
get away with thinking he held all the cards.

'Ditto,' she said tartly. 'You seemed to be having
a reasonable time yourself.'

At that he laughed. A proper laugh. His eyes spar-
kled and she hit the two-dimple jackpot.

'You're a match for me, Princess. That's for sure.
More than a match.'

'And for the last time...' she began.

'You're not a princess,' he said. 'I know. And I'll
drop it. Promise. So, we'll go to the Hamptons? Then
on to New York? We'll dress up and go out and honour my mother. And we'll tell your mother via the
world's press that her days of using you as therapist
and whipping post are done. Deal?'

'Deal,' she said, smiling.

And all the while that tinkling little bell rang in
her ears with a warning not to smile too broadly, or
feel too happy, or fall too deeply. Because there was
no one waiting to help her over these hurdles. There
never had been. And wishes didn't come true.

CHAPTER SIX

HOW MANY LEAR JETS had she flown in? Lucie wondered fleetingly as she crossed the tiny strip of Tarmac and prepared to board yet another.

The whole effort involved in being 'Party Aristocracy' as opposed to 'Dullard Aristocracy', as Lady Viv called her country cousins, seemed far too much like hard work. Apart from all the planning, the packing and the travelling, the whole angst around who would be waiting with their phone to snap a photo or record a video or—God forfend—lip-read, was just too hideous to contemplate.

Her father didn't give a damn, of course. He had been photographed and filmed and reported so many times that he'd become a bit of a caricature of himself, and was always being hunted by the press for some exploit or other. And her mother's method of second-guessing the second-guessers was simply exhausting! Why on earth either of them still felt the need to parade themselves across the world was beyond her.

Yet here she was—in jersey, sneakers, cashmere and sunglasses, a huge leather bag on her arm and a coterie of matching luggage being loaded onto the plane before her. So much for gorging on ice-cream and taking a sledgehammer to her bathroom scales. She felt a million miles apart from that girl already, she realised as she reached out for the little rail on the portable steps.

A million miles in terms of feeling like a 'woman' and of feeling in control. Had she *really* once sought comfort in clothes with elasticated waists and vats of calorific carbohydrates? Was she *honestly* the type of person who felt it vain and undignified to care if her hair was sitting nicely or if she looked her best before she greeted the world each day?

When exactly had she been transformed? she wondered. It had been so many weeks' work, and somewhere along the path she had become—what? A woman who took pride in herself? A woman who realised that although she might never be one of the petite slender blondes so beloved of the world, as Lady Viv was, she had a good mind and a healthy body and was simply being obstinate and churlish not to make best use of them?

Dante's hand touched the small of her back and the warring sensations of pleasure and anxiety sprang up, as they had every five minutes since he'd picked her up at her father's villa.

He was becoming even more tactile, she thought, pulling away without acknowledging him and climbing the short flight of steps. She really wasn't used to anyone touching her. It had simply never happened as a child, as a teenager, as an adult. She'd never sought out hugs or soothing little arm-rubs—and she didn't intend to start now. Not once did she remember climbing onto her mother's lap. And certainly no one had been there to comfort her at boarding school—apart from one awful night in the sanatorium, delirious with fever when she'd fallen into the hefty bosom of Nurse.

She could still remember the racking sobs, the sensation of her wet face on soaked cotton, of rocking and rubbing and finally the agony subsiding. But only that once. And it was a memory so painful that she never, ever aired it.

No, there hadn't been a lot of touch in her childhood. Nor a lot of love.

Even *making* love had had its challenges. Of course she'd seen enough of life to know what to expect, but it was almost a miracle that she'd rolled past the incredible urge to cut and run when he'd attempted to kiss between her legs! She couldn't explain to him why that had been so utterly unbearable. Hadn't the words in her own mind to know where to start. All she knew was that she most definitely was not and never would be able to relax enough to endure *that*.

Holding hands, nestling under an arm, exchanging starry-eyed glances…? She might just be able to pull that off this weekend. But it wasn't who she was, and she had no desire for it to be.

Cold fish? Yes. She'd been bred that way.

She walked into the cabin and settled herself into a cream leather bucket seat.

'Would you like anything, Lucie?' Dante asked, nodding to the crew, who waited at the side offering saccharine-sweet smiles as well as crystal glasses and ice and bottles galore.

'No, thank you,' she said, noting the slight edge of tension that had crept between them—or rather crept over *her* since he'd picked her up.

'Everything all right?' he asked, raising an amused eyebrow.

Of course this would be home from home for him. Making small talk after a one-night stand must be as easy as pie. She eyed him surreptitiously from under the veil of hair that cloaked her face now that she wore it down, rather in the perpetual ponytails of her youth. He was easily, breezily moving about the cabin, magnetically drawing all eyes with his innately elegant gait. Even the cabin staff in their silk blouses and tailored skirts looked like some Hollywood chorus line, gazing adoringly at the lead actor before adding their four-part harmonies.

Her mother would never have allowed that, she thought. All the staff at the castle were over the age of fifty and as broad as they were tall. And for the first time in her life Lucie really understood why. She was *jealous*—just like her mother.

'Of course.' She smiled sweetly.

She'd be damned if she would let it show.

Her coy look was rewarded by his taking her hand and leaning forward and whispering close to her ear.

'I can't wait to get you back into a bikini. Only this time there'll be no escape. You follow?'

She followed. Like a hot-heeled crab, lust scuttled over her skin as she imagined the moment when they would be alone again under a bright blue sky.

'Why don't we go and lie down right now? I'd be more than happy to get some rest if you would.'

Lucie's mind reacted with lightning speed—much more quickly than her libido.

'Not yet!' She laughed, her hand flying to her hair as she nervously checked and smoothed. 'No,' she said again, laughing as she clawed back her composure. 'Let's keep it…special.'

Dante stayed, hands braced on the armrests either side of her, bent low, his warm breath skimming her ear. She could see the honey-skinned cleft at the base of his throat and the smooth expanse of muscle that ran all the way to his navel. The faint scent of lemon and sandalwood wound around her, and the whole experience tugged her under as sure as any riptide. Lord, but resisting him took all her effort. He was supreme.

'Oh, it will be special, Princess. You can be sure of that.'

Lucie squirmed.

Wouldn't it be wonderful just to relax into this as if she were stepping into a warm bath? Suddenly the urge to scrub away all the hang-ups she had was overpowering. How many more times was she going to get a chance like this?

She raised her eyes up to his steady, twinkling gaze.

'I have absolutely no doubt.'

He grinned. *Wow.*

'Keep your hands where I can see them, mister!' she said, in a fake American accent.

'Won't be a problem,' he said.

He dipped his head and kissed her very, very carefully. His lips were warm and firm and smooth and wonderful. He didn't move a muscle—only his lips. She felt herself let go, just a tiny bit, slipping down a little in the seat, letting her head fall back and her lips rise up. He continued. His tongue slipped in on the soft sigh she breathed out and he lifted his hands from the chair to her jaw. Then slowly, never stopping his sensual oral caress, he lifted her up.

They stood aligned. Bodies pressed against one another. His hands cupped her face and her mouth was supplicant under his. She didn't want to stop this. She *couldn't* stop this.

His body and her body and her mouth and his mouth were all she knew. Her hands found his chest, the smooth cotton of his shirt over hard, strong muscle. She slid them round, feeling the layer of muscle beside his ribs, then on to his back. She felt the deep indentations of his backbone, the welt of muscle on either side, all the way down to the base of his spine and—oh, her hands fell even lower as she palmed his very fabulous buttocks.

Suddenly her hands were stopped, grabbed by the wrists.

'Keep your hands where I can see 'em, Princess.' He smiled as he kissed the corner of her mouth, her cheek, her ear. She squirmed out of reach and he moved back to her mouth.

There was nothing she wanted to do more than continue to feel those kisses, to rub her aching nipples against his hard body. He held her wrists in a strong grip, bringing his body into even closer contact with hers, so the long, hard ridge of his erection was imprinted on her stomach.

'Dante…' she sighed.

'I'll keep it special—I promise. Let's go.'

In one swift move he spun her round so she was marching ahead of him towards a door at the back of the cabin. She was supremely aware of the swollen lips between her legs, rubbing and throbbing with every step, but she welcomed it. Welcomed it as much as the firm pressure round each wrist and the knowledge that he was right behind her, helping her, pushing her out of this repressed fortress she'd built.

They got to the door and he reached past her to open it. Neat, elegant, compact—the room was exactly as it should be—but she had no time for detail.

Behind her the strong, safe presence of Dante pushed on. The door closed.

She faced the bed, heard the door click and felt his hands on her shoulders. She gave a tiny jump—she couldn't help herself.

'Hey...'

He stepped closer—she could feel his warmth, his strength. She could sink back and lose herself in it. Couldn't she? It would be so lovely... But she'd stopped and thought for too long, let her brain take over, and all that mental chatter had started up again.

He can't really find you that attractive—you're nothing special...nothing like those other girls.

She felt his hands slide around her, skim her ribs, cup her breasts, flick over her nipples.

She flinched. Her hands jumped to his arms as he stepped forward.

'Sensitive? Perfect,' he whispered, and he stepped right up and welded himself to her back.

And then there was nowhere to go, nothing to think or do except just to *be*. His fingers trailed sinful little circles over her skin and the blaze of lust returned, burning up all the worries in her head. There was nothing but that feeling, those daring fingers circling and extending the pleasure, sensing her anticipation. It was going to hurt any second now. Building and aching and soothing and gorgeous. Relentless. And of course it wouldn't hurt—it was too perfect.

Her hands lay on his forearms, as limp as the

folds of silk that skirted the bed. Her head flopped back and her breath was stolen away on a whisper of pleasure.

He stepped in to extinguish the final layer of air between them and she felt him. Hard and pressing. She wanted that feeling all over again. She wanted that sense of oblivion that only he could deliver. She wanted to lie in his arms as a naked offering. She wanted to be worshipped and to worship. And she didn't care that her thighs were pale and wobbly or that her tummy stuck out. She could let go—she could...she *really* could.

'You're amazing, Lucie,' he said, sliding his hand—finally!—under the layer of waterfall cashmere, under the thick cotton shirt to the fine silk of her bra. His fingers tugged the cups down and rubbed mercilessly at nipples she was sure were going to combust with the unstinting pleasure.

She had no will to argue. He could say what he wanted as long as he never stopped.

'Amazing...but far too overdressed.'

He spun her round, unhooked her bra, and groaned his own pleasure as her breasts fell heavily into his hands.

'You *kill* me,' he said, lifting her layers and peeling them up over her head. 'I try—I really try to take things easy. And slow. But one look at you and—see the state you've got me in again?'

He glanced down, indicating the huge bulge in his jeans.

The chill of the air-conditioned cabin prickled her bare skin. She stared at him and he laughed, lifting her hand and putting it right on him.

'Wow!' she said, laughing back and relishing the sensation of hot, hard flesh pushing against soft denim for release.

'Yes, *wow*,' he said, his tone changing. Becoming low, with an unmistakable curl of command. 'But first I want to see you on that bed.'

He reached his hands forward and followed them immediately with his mouth, latching on to a darkly pink distended nipple and tugging with his tongue.

She called out her pleasure, so intense was the glorious feeling, and felt herself fall back onto the bed. His hands were at the waistband of her leggings. She kicked off her sneakers. He tugged. Pulled the dark jersey down and with them her panties, exposing the dark golden curls at her apex.

His head bent and instantly she scissored away, her legs jerking as she rolled onto her side.

'No, please don't do that! I really *wouldn't* like it, you know.'

'Honey, there's not a woman alive who doesn't like it. And I want to do it for you.'

He grabbed her hip with one hand and tugged her free of her garments.

In a heartbeat she was naked on the bed and on her back. Her legs were still open as she scuttled to get some distance. How on earth could he want to put his mouth *there*? She wasn't built for that kind of attention. It was horrifying—she would never subject anyone to that.

But even as those chattering hateful voices loomed louder again in her mind he was tearing off his clothes and kicking off his shoes and lying beside her, his smooth golden skin so warm beside her own cloudy pale flesh. And that huge, thick thrust of his manhood— She reached out instinctively.

'Not yet—not until you've let me do what I want to you.'

'Dante, please—please don't do that.'

He slid over her, braced himself and looked down as she stared up anxiously into his face. She drew her knees up and knotted them under his body.

But he merely laughed and lay down beside her, hooked his elbow and settled his head into his hand, all the while looking at her with a faint one-dimple smile.

'You're a puzzle…but a very beautiful one.'

And he trailed a finger from her chin downwards, firm and fatally lighting up a path between her breasts and down further, slowing at her abdomen. She lay still as a corpse, loving the pleasure he gave her and hating her own stupid reactions. Here she was, about to join the mile-high club, and she was still trying to talk herself out of it.

'Lucie?'

She glanced up into that face. God, but he was outrageously handsome. He lifted his finger and hooked her chin, holding her face tilted while he flicked on another dimple.

'Are you listening to me?'

He tugged her chin, forcing her to nod. She giggled. He grinned.

'Repeat after me: *I am a beautiful woman and I will let my lover take pleasure in my beauty.*'

'I am a— Oh, heavens, Dante, don't be so ridiculous. I'm not saying that.'

'What part of it?'

He leaned up over her now, looming like a Greek god gazing at his mortal plaything.

'The stuff that's full of BS, baby!' she said, in her fake American accent, desperately trying to make light of this and squirming away even as he lowered himself onto her, pinning her to the bed.

His erection jabbed at her and he laughed again, positioning himself between her legs. Instantly she relaxed, hooked her legs around his back and urged him in.

'You're such a little tease, Princess—but there's no main course until we've had the starters.'

He dipped and kissed her. Gentle, sensual and slow. She felt herself sink back further into the bed.

'You're so kissable. Beautiful,' he said, sliding his tongue and tangling it with hers.

She moaned, relishing the sensation of his lips moulding to hers. His hand skimmed her thigh, her waist, cupped her breast and stroked.

'Your body is all-woman… Lucie, your *curves*— you should love these lush, lovely curves.'

He kissed her nipple and began to move further down her body, but tension surged again.

'No, please—'

He returned to her mouth, but slid his hand down, gripped her hip and eased onto his side, lying alongside her, his lips and tongue licking and lapping and loving her mouth. This was perfect—this was what she wanted. If only he would stay like this.

And then his expert fingers touched her throbbing little bud and she jumped.

He smothered her moans with his mouth. 'Relax, let me do this for you.'

And even if she'd wanted to there was no way she could have stopped it. She needed it. *Desperately.*

On and on he kissed her, and gently rubbed exactly where she needed to be rubbed. Moans filled the room. *Her* voice. Louder and louder. She wondered absently if anyone could hear her, and her mind flooded with images of the chorus line cabin girls.

And then the incredible peak she was climbing vanished, and all there was was this room, this bed, this man. And then all her worries began to pop up again, choking her pleasure, allowing self-consciousness to seep back in.

'Hey, Lucie…'

As if he knew, he pulled her back, kissed her more deeply, filled her head with just one feeling—

making love. And she was back on the track, on the
peak, surmounting all the chatter and the faces and
the anxiety.

'Now, Lucie. Come for me. *Now.*'

His voice was filled with authority, and his fingers
crazily, expertly tuned her like an instrument. Her
body was unable to resist and her mind cleared—she
felt herself sail over the edge. And she screamed, released. His fingers still worked on her and she craved
and yearned and flew with the joy of it.

'Sweetheart, that was beautiful. You *beautiful*
girl.'

He hugged her close and rocked them together for
moments long and lovely. Slowly she settled back
into her body, easing into his gentle hold. She could
easily be held like this. For ever.

Her eyes flew open and she pushed him away,
wondering if she'd said that out loud! Good grief,
she was all over the place. *For ever?* There was no
'for ever' about this! This was most definitely 'for
now'. She was the newly sexually confident lover
of a man with a reputation as long as her arm. She
wasn't going to fall for him, for heaven's sake! She
wasn't *that* stupid.

But she needn't have worried. Even as she pushed
out of his hold he was moving her round, and in
one sure move he had eased himself right where he
wanted to be. Lucie was bruised, she was tender,
and she knew having his huge thrusting penis inside
her was going to make her even more so, but all the

voices were silenced. Her body was in control and it was clear and unequivocal. She *would* have him, and she would have him *now*.

So much pleasure—*so* much! Her mind cleared. There was nothing she could possibly do other than make love to this man. Her body was just her body, and all it could do was receive him.

'Oh, Dante,' she heard herself say, and her arms threaded around his back, sealing him closer to her, absorbing the swell and roll of muscle as he pushed himself in and out. Suddenly he was building to his own climax and, just knowing that, she tumbled again too.

He lay on her, panting, and she held him close, closed her eyes, squeezed every last moment, every gorgeous sensation. Her hand cupped the back of his head, felt sweat on his neck, and she smiled at that.

'I think you're getting the hang of things,' he said, suddenly lifting himself off and away.

He moved into the bathroom and closed the door without a backward glance.

Lucie opened her eyes, stared at the shadows that danced on the cabin's low ceiling. She heard the jet's harsh thrum and felt the steadily slowing beat of her heart. Under her the world was falling away, the oceans and islands thousands of feet below vanishing into a blue haze. And before her the sky was cloudless and clear and vast.

Dante had emboldened her. She'd lived more in the past two days than she'd done in the past two decades. But there were no illusions. None. The ink was barely dry on their contract and already she was seeing warning signs in the small print. Had she been more than a little naïve to think that she would be able to come out of it the same way she went in?

Probably. But being a cold fish had never been *this* much fun.

CHAPTER SEVEN

NEWS TRAVELLED FAST. A quiet couple of days in his house in East Hampton? Well, that was never going to happen. There were a dozen messages on his private line when he got to the house, as well as the usual assault of unsolicited texts offering all sorts of business. And all sorts of fun. It was as if they could sniff him coming in on the air before the helicopter even landed.

There was a time when he'd shied away from the tractor beam of adoration that followed him around the polo circuit—particularly since Rocco had taken himself off the field. But now he was cool with it. They were just looking for a leader—someone to follow, someone to idolise. All nonsense, but who was he to disabuse anyone of their dreams?

So when the polo club's land here had been parcelled up and sold off, and the diehards had wanted a replacement, he'd known he was in for another flood of offers he couldn't refuse. They saw him as a polo blue-blood—which, despite Her Ladyship's view, he was…like it or not. Yes, it seemed everyone saw him as some kind of elite.

Except her.

He chuckled to himself as he walked across the tennis court. It was too hot for tennis. Or rather *she* was too hot for tennis. His plans for Lady Lucie ran to something needing far fewer clothes.

Normally he'd have called Marco as soon as he'd fixed his schedule. Marco had become even more of a brother than Rocco—he was a local Montauk boy, born and bred, and in the long hot summers of his late youth they'd roamed the coasts and forests together. It had always been a wrench, leaving here to go back to Argentina. And school. Even after school there had been times when he'd nearly packed it all in and come up here to live permanently—but he hadn't wanted to involve anyone else in his mess. It had been *his* creation and *his* responsibility.

He was glad now that he'd handled the whole thing himself. He'd despise himself even more if anyone knew—especially someone like Marco, who'd been pretty much a constant for the last fifteen years and had been through his own tough times…way tougher than Dante's.

He'd be a bit more than bemused when he learned that Dante had finally arrived, with a woman in tow, and hadn't contacted him. He bent to pick up a lone tennis ball from the ash and lobbed it over the net, aiming for the fencepost beyond. Bullseye! He might have lost some of his mind, but at least he hadn't lost his vision.

This just never happened. East Hampton boys ran together and played together. They played tennis and surfed and rode and chased girls. It was what they always did. And Dante liked being one of the boys very much.

But here he was, in his very private home, with his soon to be very public mistress. And when he'd landed not only had he turned his phone to silent, he'd tossed it into a drawer and pretty much checked out of society for two days.

Two days left. Call him competitive, but he was determined to melt every last drop of his ice maiden before they hit Fifth Avenue and the next gruelling part of his schedule. A man with more sense would have walked away as soon as he'd recognised that uneasy, queasy feeling in his gut—a feeling he'd last felt fifteen years ago, just before life had hit the buffers—but the thought of walking away from Lucie Bond was like a hungry man walking away from an all-day diner. Why *would* he?

He was barely thirty. He had years before he had to get all down and dirty with analysts and accountants. Who wanted that kind of life? He loved to play polo. He loved his women. He had so much more fun to have before he needed to have daily massages to get the knots out of his neck—didn't he?

His decision to get involved in the polo club's real estate drama had been inevitable. He had felt

the change in the wind, had tasted the sobering fla-
vours of real business brewing in some corporate
cauldron that he was being drawn closer and closer
to. But that didn't mean he had to hang up his dancing shoes completely. Not yet, anyway.

He'd nearly completed his daily circuit—one of
his little habits when he was here. Just checking it
was all still there, with nothing that needed his im-
mediate attention. He had staff—of course he did.
But no one knew these grounds as he did. His parents had long since moved on and bought a much
smaller property over on Bridgehampton, but this
old place was in his blood.

Which made it all the more interesting that he had
permitted himself to share it with Lucie.

He skirted the formal topiary garden that his
mother had had planted. He couldn't recall her ever
spending any time in it when it had been finished,
but that was pretty much the way with Eleanor.
'Next' was her mantra. She had her projects, and
occasionally they involved the family, but more often
than not they didn't.

He wasn't sore about it—he'd long since accepted
that having a high-achieving mother wasn't the same
as having a stay-at-home mother. And her life was
her choice, nobody else's. Good for her—he was
proud of her. And he'd be clapping harder than anyone when she walked up and took that award on
Saturday night.

He walked up the side of the lap pool and around

the side of the east wing as the late-afternoon sun beat down through a couple of cheerful clouds. A few more minutes and he'd be clear of the shelter of the trees and would be able to hear the ever-satisfying sound of breakers crashing. And find Lucie.

He'd left her sitting on a lounger under a huge umbrella with a cup of tea and a phone. She was going to call her mother and start to put down some long-overdue boundaries.

He cornered the house and stepped down onto the wide pebbled path, still screened by a high flank of hedging—and there she was.

He stopped.

It was just like the moment when he'd first seen her.

She was standing on the edge of the terrace that wrapped around the house. The loungers, parasols, tables and chairs in all shapes and forms were behind her. Her head was high and her chin was proud. She stood staring out over the bay like a queen surveying her fleet. The wind whipped at her hair and she lifted a hand to hold it back from her face.

And in that moment he was struck—just as he'd been that first time. She was *regal*. In every sense of the word. She commanded respect and it gnawed at a part of him to think that others might not treat her well. And worst of all herself.

She had a depth and quality that he'd rarely come across. But she was so hung up on what people thought and couldn't see that it didn't matter a damn. Well, everyone had their crosses to bear—she'd figure herself out in time.

'Hey, Lucie!' He started his ambling again. There was no rush. They had days yet. It was the Hamptons...they were on a holiday—life was cool.

She turned slowly and, one hand held up to her eyes, shielding her gaze from the sun, let a smile spread across her face.

'Hey,' he said again as he restarted on his path towards her. 'How's it going? Did you get through to her? I mean, did you get your *message* through to her?'

She looked away and her smile faded as if someone had sucked the warmth from summer—just at the mention of her mother, that stupid, selfish woman. But she gathered herself—it was almost palpable. She looked strained, and then her smile was back in place.

For a heartbeat he hoped it was he who'd put it there. But, no, there was no mileage in those kinds of thoughts. He never allowed himself dumb daydreams like that. Because that was all it would be—one short, sugary dream, ending in decay.

Celine di Rosso had shown him the pain of love—and loss. And he would happily leave that to one side, thank you very much. He wasn't going to say it would never happen. It might in another couple of decades. Maybe. If he needed a wife to partner him at tedious dinner parties or on turgid cruises. Someone to tell him to trim his eyebrows or cut back on the beers.

You're not my type.

Thank God she felt the same way. He grinned, watching her pick her way down from the terrace to the tree-lined path to join him. Here she came— the woman who'd crushed his ego. But being told he didn't cut it for her had been the best news he could imagine. It guaranteed him a fantastic week of fun and sex and good company, with none of the usual 'relationship' dread. No speech. No guilt gift. Nothing but a mutually agreeable, time-limited private party.

Perfect. Absolutely *perfect*.

'Hello,' she said, pausing at the top of the steps and looking at him in that faintly bemused way.

'Hello, Princess,' he said back.

And before she could scowl he hopped up the three steps, grabbed her and kissed her. *Hard.*

She squealed and laughed. She pushed at him. Pathetically. And then she let herself go, the way she always did, and melted into him on a sigh. Another jagged clump of ice gone.

'So...' he said, pulling back and watching as her eyes slowly opened. All the little flecks of moss-green were surrounded by a darker ring of olive. There were smoky smudges under her lids, and the full swollen pout of her lips, unadorned with any make-up, tasted like a woman should taste. 'So you called your mother?'

She stepped back, and again her head began to dip.

He hooked her chin. Lifted it up and eyed her carefully. 'And...? How did it go?'

She tossed her head, pushed her shoulders back and stuck out her chin. He wondered again how many times she'd practised that particular little time-buying routine. In the face of questions about herself or anyone close to her she shut down, became imperial.

'All fine, yes. Everything is fine at home—well, as fine as it ever is. So,' she said breezily, 'did you get in touch with your friend? Are you *really* going to drag me out of this wonderful lair and into the spotlight?'

They took the steps to the beach together, flanked by the sun-splashed high white walls of the house and the curve of lawn that had seen more than its fair share of brotherly tussles and fights over the years.

'You'll bloom in the spotlight.'

'I *hate* the spotlight,' she said, rolling her eyes. 'You saw that—you saw what I'm like.'

'It'll only be a few friends.' He laughed. 'Nothing major. No grand prizes to call. You won't need to throw yourself overboard. Consider it a dress rehearsal for the awards ceremony.'

Lucie slowed. 'I suppose you're right. I won't be quite as bad as I was at the auction—big crowds are definitely the worst. But I'm still a Shrinking Violet. I *hate* being the centre of any attention—whatsoever.'

'I get it,' he said. 'I think… But haven't you had training or counselling or something to get you past this? Surely part of the package of being a member of the aristocracy is getting out there, meeting people?'

'Yes, of course, for some. But I've never had to do much of it. My mother normally takes care of that side of things. I hang back. One might even say I've been encouraged to—which suits me fine. I've tried hypnosis, and I've tried therapy, but the only thing that really works for me is deep breathing. And that's only if I'm in small groups. Public speaking? Forget it. I've *never* got over that.'

She smiled round at him, fleetingly.

Dante shot her a glance, a smile, a squeeze.

'You'll be great tonight—no speeches. In fact you'll be lucky to get a word in edgeways,' he said, thinking of the crowd that would be gathering at Betty's.

They'd be intrigued that he'd brought anyone at all, and the fact that she was a member of the British aristocracy—however minor—would be an added attraction. But they *knew* him. They knew better than to read anything into it.

There seemed to be no end of bars and restaurants in East Hampton. Grills, seafood, Italian, fusion. Chic, contemporary, bright, moody. All perfectly hideous, as far as Lucie could tell. With every passing minute in the car her appetite had decreased in direct proportion to their proximity to their destination.

Dante's friend—or rather Dante's *best* friend—Marco, was hosting a 'little get-together' at Betty's Kitchen—an old, established restaurant in an old, established clapboard house.

The things she now knew about Betty's Kitchen!

Dante had loved to go there as a child. Marco's cousin was the owner and it was incredibly well-patronised. The waiting list for a table for 'un-knowns' stretched for months. And apparently the chowder was unmatched in the whole of The Hamptons.

Lucie was quite sure all of that was true, but she had very little desire to find out for herself. And the thought of a 'little get-together' with almost a dozen new faces was something that made even the word 'chowder' stick in her throat like an unswallowed mouthful of whale blubber.

Dante sat beside her, one hand on the wheel, one hand on her thigh. As if at any moment she might leap from the car.

She looked down at his fingers, searching for some sign of imperfection in this crucifyingly perfect man. Truly, there was nothing. His fingers were long but strong, with flat, smooth nails. His hands were broad, with an appropriate scattering of bronzed hair starting at the outside edge and leading to his wrist. Veins stood out proudly, healthily. His grip was heavy and sure.

She sighed, thinking of the things he had done, the things he could do with those hands. Soothing her, pleasuring her, but most of all imbuing her with such a sense of calm and peace when he held her own hand in his.

As they'd walked hand in hand back from the shore to the house earlier, each holding their shoes in their free hand, she'd felt such a strange, such a beautiful feeling.

Why? She couldn't say. As beaches went it was lovely. But she'd been on better. As summer days went it was nice. Warm, slightly breezy and fresh. But for some reason the whole thing—the slide of water on her wet feet, their race up from the water's edge to dry off, the worm casts and gull cries and the steady, rhythmic motion of the lapping water, the ebb and flow of life—had struck her in that moment.

Such a beautiful moment. Such a treasured memory. She'd known that even as it had faded. Even as they'd stepped away from the soft swell of each broken wave…even as their feet had splashed in the little pools left behind in the ridged sand. As Dante had held her hand and they'd walked silently away from the air that had been filled with her happy cries and his deep laughter mere minutes earlier.

He had turned just as she had, and they'd shared a smile. Just that. A single smile.

Lucie's throat closed and her eyes smarted for a moment at the thought. How strange that a beautiful memory could reduce her to tears. She quickly lifted her head, stared out at the passing scenery, blanked her mind and breathed from her diaphragm. In and out and all would be well. The last thing she needed to be was weepy about silly things like walks on the beach! Not when she had all these other things swimming about in her head.

Her mother, for one thing. Well, she couldn't be faulted for trying! And using a new angle this time. Gone was the, *Don't you dare!* approach, and in its place was, *Have your heard the rumours?*

Apparently Dante was the worst womaniser on the planet. He had never had a girlfriend for longer than three months. He was always in the coolest nightclubs, with the coolest people. With men who were just like him and girls who drank only champagne and ate only with their eyes. Oh, and finally—his adopted brother was a thug with a terrible past and no breeding whatsoever.

Lucie had shut her up at that point. She'd been able to hear the shrill desperation, the need for control, but she absolutely would not listen to her mother passing judgement on people she'd never even met.

People like Dante, whose hand now gently squeezed her thigh. She turned her head to look at him just as he gave her a sun-bright wink. And her heart nearly stopped beating in her chest.

'What is it?' she almost snapped at him. It really was unhelpful that he was just so heart-stoppingly handsome.

'Hey, don't go getting all icy on me now, Princess. You've been sweet all evening and we're almost there.'

He pressed another squeeze to her leg and rubbed it. Then lifted his hand and placed it back on the steering wheel as he began to turn the car into a car park lot. Lucie looked around at the dozen or so cars lined up on either side of the picket fence and the sign with curlicue letters picked out in red, reading 'Betty's Kitchen'.

'Well, here we are. And it looks like Marco's here already.' Dante nodded to a gleaming motorbike parked right at the front of the steps. 'Sounds like he's here already too,' he said, as a chorus of laughter erupted and carried all the way out to the car park.

Lucie's fingers fumbled on the seatbelt clasp, but in seconds Dante had opened her door, unclipped her and helped her up from the low bucket seat.

He slid her a smile and cocked his head as she smoothed her skirt and tried to tug it down an inch or so past the wobbly flesh above her knees.

'What are you doing that for? You've got fantastic legs,' he said, stilling her and giving her a bemused look. 'Come on.'

He took her hand and on they walked—five steps up and a short stroll past red-shuttered windows that opened onto a white deck offering glimpses of intimate tables and elegant bodies. The quiet, convivial buzz of conversation and clinks of glassware and tableware melted into the early-evening air.

'There he is!'

A girl's voice—American west coast, and positively brimming with confidence. Lucie felt her stomach lurch. The glossy black doors, pinned back with brass latches, were right in front of her now and there was nowhere else to go but forward.

Lucie's feet faltered.

'Dante—*baby!*'

In the gloom of the restaurant she could make out a polished floor, tables covered in white linen with fresh bowls of flowers, candles and glasses all catching the light, and there at the back one single long table. Her eyes landed there, on the dark-haired man who sat at the centre with a broad smile and a hand raised. And the sleek-limbed lovelies who sat all around him, each dress shorter than the next.

She steeled herself. It was just a restaurant...they were just people. No one was going to die and there was every chance she would have a nice time.

She found her breath and followed it for a moment.

From the corner of her eye she could see a man in black trousers and shirt approach them. He smiled broadly and gestured them inside.

'How lovely to see you, Dante. It's been too long. And you've brought a friend...'

Lucie felt herself being gently shoved forward.

'You're with me. You're beautiful. You're going to have a great time.'

Words whispered close to her ear, but instead of shivering she absorbed them.

'Gino, hey—thanks!' Dante strode past her but clasped her hand as he moved and tugged her along in his wake. 'This is my friend Lady Lucinda Bond. Though I reckon she'll let you call her Lucie.'

Smooth and sure, he slid his arm around her waist and kept them both moving inside, shaking the maître d's hand as he went and steering them through the room to the table at the back.

In a haze of air the slimmest, sleekest limbs and the shiniest, longest hair she had ever seen appeared—all swarming and air-kissing around Dante, with wide, perfect smiles and sooty-rimmed eyes. One after the other they paid homage and then slowly sat down, folding their limbs like retractable weapons and lifting glasses to their lips.

'And you must be Lucie!' The swarthy dark-eyed man who was clearly holding court beamed. He stood. A few faces turned at the noise of his chair scraping on the floor. He began to walk round the table and she could feel a bristle of energy.

'This must be and is Lady Lucinda Bond of Strathdee. Play nice, now, Marco.'

Suddenly she felt like a package at some silly show-and-tell event. She wasn't going to let herself down!

She tossed her hair back and lifted her chin. Thrust out her hand. 'Your reputation precedes you, Marco. Though one rather hopes it's undeserved.'

For a moment there was complete silence. And then she heard Dante's unmistakable chuckle. And the high-pitched titter of girls. Everybody seemed to be staring from her to Marco and back again.

'Well, I never thought I'd see you lost for words, man.'

He slapped his friend on the back, moved past him and pulled out a chair for Lucie. She sat down with a curt thank you and looked round the table. Marco took his place and everything started up again. Champagne glasses were lifted to lips and bottles of beer were clinked together.

Lucie's heart pounded in her ears. What on earth had prompted her to say that? She'd tried to be funny but it just hadn't worked. Why was she so gauche? Why couldn't she just relax when she met people? It was either a full-blown panic attack or…just an attack! She'd give anything to be able to smile and speak and act like a normal human being. And she had very little time before she'd have to go through it all over again. It had seemed such a good idea when he had suggested it, but now that the awards were mere days away, thqt mental chatter was really starting up.

'I'll take that one for the team, buddy. As long as you take ten minutes out of your…*ahem*…very busy private life to get this deal finally moving.'

A shadow passed over Dante's face. Swiftly, almost imperceptibly. But then he was back. He nodded. 'I read over the reports. And I guess I'm going to have to make the move some day.'

'Is that a yes?'

'It is,' said Dante, with a grin breaking right over his face.

Marco beamed. 'You'll never regret it. And the community here will never forget it. Honestly, I can't tell you how proud I am. This is massive Dante. *Huge.* Not only the investment, but the fact that you're prepared to make Little Hauk your base. I can't tell you what that means to me professionally. And personally.'

Dante nodded slowly. He looked directly at Lucie, those blue lasers finding their target easily.

Marco was still droning on. 'Well, that's part one of the master plan in place. All you need now is the picket fence and the beautiful wife and you'll be home free.' He laughed. 'More champagne anyone?'

And the words circled the air, causing all sorts of images to flare and then float.

Dante settled down? Married?

'I don't think you need any more to drink, buddy. My master plan has no space for your drunken hallucinations. Not any time in *this* millennium, that's for sure.'

A pause hung over the table like a thick cloud of smog.

'Aw, come on—we all know it's only a matter of time before you're down on one knee, begging some poor woman to marry you. God help her.'

The air crackled with laughter at Marco's comeback. Lucie touched her hair, fingered her earring, tugged her skirt down. She lifted her napkin and spread it out on her lap. The menu, in an old leather cover, stood lopsided, leaning on an ice bucket. She picked it up, pressed it flat onto the white plate before her.

Set Menu for Dinner... Starters... Entrees... Specials of the House.

She flicked the laminated pages and read the words, determined to erase the ones she had just heard spoken out loud. Even though she'd said she didn't want anything from him after this week, she suddenly realised that it hurt to know that she would never be a part of Dante's master plan.

CHAPTER EIGHT

'THE PLAN IS that we'll pass Sag Harbour Marina, fly along the Long Island Gold Coast, take a little tourist tour of Manhattan and land after about forty minutes. In time for lunch. How does that sound?'

Lucie clicked her belt closed, touched her headphones and nodded with a smile to Dante.

'Yeah? Okay?'

She made a thumbs-up sign and turned to look out at the landscape that was disappearing below her into a Toytown model of waterways, hedges, pools and matchbox mansions.

She'd only been there three days and at one thousand feet in the air above it already felt wistful for the place. Again she wondered at herself. She'd been in fabulous locations all over the world. Palaces, yachts, secluded villas tucked away on their own private islands. From her earliest memories she'd been away for weekends here and there, dragged about to parties and holidays in luxury locations that most people couldn't even dream of. Even her own idyllic Petit

Pierre—her heaven on earth, the home that she normally pined for from the moment she left it until she arrived back, where she discarded her worries and woes and wrapped herself up in a warm, wonderful world—didn't feel quite so amazing as this stretch of island dotted with green, blue and brown.

She could dwell on that, let the mental chatter increase to deafening proportions, or she could simply let herself be swept along in the next few hours of what Dante had promised would be 'interesting' times.

She stole a glance at him, piloting the helicopter, making it look like the easiest thing on earth. He did that with most things, of course. It was something in the way he held himself—his shoulders were always low, never tensed, never hunched. Or was it the way he moved—as if every part of him was tuned and oiled, supple and strong? The way he held her eyes when he spoke. Or listened. The way he held her hand.

Held her hand.

Who would have thought that jumpy, jittery Lucie could stand to have someone hold her hand? Now, *that* was a miracle itself. But there were more miracles to come—he had promised her.

She knew exactly what he was referring to. And he had been incredibly patient with her. But there was only so far she could allow her intimacy with him to go. No matter how gentle, how tender, how sensitive he'd been, she still couldn't relax enough to allow him full access to her body.

'All in good time—no need to get anxious,' he'd said. And she'd said it was hardly worth bothering about.

But she knew and he knew that it was just one more in a long series of hang-ups that were holding her back. When those voices started their chattering in her head, their deafening anxious phrases going on and on, bringing her further and further down, she knew she was slipping back.

And when she felt that finger under her chin, lifting it up, and saw those eyes beaming into hers—well, that was all very well. He had a vested interest in keeping the party going. But when Dante went back to his life, his season in Dubai, and then moved back to Little Hauk to start up this new polo foundation—well, where would Lucie be? Tagging turtles. Dodging phone calls. Hiding.

'Okay?' he asked again, his voice resonating through the headphones, making her jump.

'Yes.' She smiled back as he slipped her a conspiratorial wink.

'See that place down there—?' He pointed to a huge sprawling series of buildings, a pool half-empty and green with moss, hard-baked brown earth and grass that hurt. Of course it had its own jetty, as all these huge places had—Little Hauk included. She looked round at Dante questioningly.

'That was Marco's family's place. Until his father gambled away every last cent and his mother upped and offed.'

Lucie looked back at the enormous rambling estate, sitting in the dust, surrounded by immaculate properties to the left, to the right and behind it, and the ocean in front. To think the swarthy, happy guy who'd held court with Dante, good-naturedly sparring with him, had been brought up there. It was easily the biggest landmass of prime real estate she had ever seen. They must have been immensely rich, even by her standards.

But he had no side. No airs. No graces. Just like Dante.

'Big, isn't it?' said the muffled voice in her ears. 'Just goes to show that there's nothing you can rely on in this world but yourself. Marco learned that the hard way. It's his dream to buy it back—to clear the family name. And I don't think it will be too long either.'

Lucie nodded at that. She'd learned last night that Marco had built up several local businesses, and that it had been his sheer willpower that had resulted in their dream of the polo foundation. And now he and Dante would be partners he was probably well on the way to making his dream come true.

What was *Lucie's* dream? What was *she* going to do to bring honour on her family? Could her family and her home be taken away? It had never even occurred to her that she might be anything other than Lady Lucinda Bond of Strathdee. It was like air and earth—the granite of the castle and the waters of Petit Pierre. It was unconscionable that the day might come when everything that defined her would go.

As mansion upon mansion passed beneath them in a blur she suddenly felt a sense of panic. What if it *did* all go? What if one day the privilege and the money vanished? If her father's title became no more than a piece of paper, with no power, pomp or even circumstance. What if she had nowhere to hide any more?

Baseball fields, an airport and then the towers of Manhattan appeared. She barely noticed them, so caught up was she in the thoughts rampaging through her mind.

She'd never once considered being anything other than Lady Lucinda Bond, and one day Duchess of Strathdee. And had never really been remotely grateful for it either. She'd spent such an age privately bemoaning the fact that she had two decadent, indolent parents and hadn't once appreciated the fact that were it not for them she wouldn't have so much as a bean to spend. The castle in Scotland, the villa, the yacht, the annual income… None of that she had earned herself.

Her father's choices and her mother's choices were what they were. She shouldn't worry about them—she should be out there following her own dream. Tagging turtles, dodging phone calls and hiding? They weren't her dreams—they were holding tasks. Things to do to kill time.

She looked at Dante. He *never* bemoaned his mother. He never spoke about any of his family in anything other than glowing tones.

She could read between the lines, of course—when he described all his mother's achievements she got the sense of a woman who spent more time fixing other people's problems than attending to her own family. There were only so many hours in the day, and if she was spending them with other people's children who was spending time with hers?

But he was silently, resolutely loyal. No cracks showed in that family. And, though Lucie had never breathed a word of her own views about her parents to anyone other than Dante, the world could see by her actions that she wanted nothing to do with any of them.

It was time she grew up, stopped feeling sorry for herself and began to appreciate the gifts life had given her instead of taking it for granted and whining all the time.

'Central Park Reservoir,' said the voice in her ears, and she looked out across the vista of flat and jagged roofed towers in every shade of brown and beige, like a meadow filled with stumpy corncobs. And there sat the park, sunk down like some huge mossy stepping stone, with the flat blue puddle of the reservoir in the middle. 'Almost there.'

Dante tipped up his visor and winked and Lucie beamed right back. He had gone out on a limb, inviting her to this awards dinner. She knew that now—

she could tell how important it was to him, despite how easily he played it down. He wouldn't want to upset anyone—least of all his mother—and there was no way that Lucie was going to get all needy on him. There would be no panic attacks, no blubbing, no fainting. Nothing but head up, chest out and onwards. She wouldn't be anything other than the perfect guest.

'One hour and we'll be sitting down to lunch in one of Manhattan's finest. And twelve hours after that we'll be through with this and we can both get back to our lives.'

He winked again, but this time the smile that Lucie returned was fixed. It was painted. It was fake.

'Bet you can't wait,' he said, widening his grin. Then he tipped down his visor and turned back to the job in hand.

Dante felt like a heel.

He gripped the collective lever and gave the helicopter another burst of speed as she banked to the left. The truth was that he couldn't wait for this whole thing to be over. It was getting under his skin like a third degree burn, and he was beginning to feel that he might need more than a cold compress to get through it.

He'd known as soon as Marco had made that stupid comment about picket fences and pretty wives that something had clicked in her head. He could have cheerfully reached across and strangled him, punched him, thrown him into the bay as shark bait.

His fingers gripped the control as he straightened up and settled himself down. He had less than twenty minutes before they came face to face with the formidable force of nature that was his mother. And then the toughest part of the gig—coming right up.

He should have thought this through a whole lot better. He should have seen it coming. Hell, a blind idiot would have seen it coming. Lucie was perfect for him. That was what his mother was going to conclude after about—oh, a nanosecond in her company. And even if he sent her an affidavit right now, got a restraining order, or even a gag, she would still manipulate the conversation round to suit her way of thinking.

Yes, she wanted her son married off. It was untidy otherwise. He was like a rope lying about that somebody could trip themselves up on.

Yes, he had to be married—but not just to anybody! Oh, no, someone with class, with pedigree. Someone beautiful, intelligent, witty and warm. Yes, Lucie was absolutely perfect for him. And for that reason she had to be told in no uncertain terms that their hot week in the Hamptons was a one-time, never to be repeated *ever* event.

He snatched a quick glance at her but she was sitting immobile, staring out at the scenery. He so badly wanted to be wrong about the whole 'picket fence' thing, but he knew in his heart of hearts how she'd looked when she'd heard those words. He'd seen it so many times before. That flare of an imagined future. Some crazy vision of them together that was just never going to happen. He'd spelled it out in words of one syllable…

So—he pressed his foot to the floor to turn—there would be today, then tonight, and then the final love scene. And then the wobbly lip while suitcases were packed and off they went.

Pity. She was as close to perfect as anyone had ever been.

But nobody was. *Nobody.* And didn't the fact that she had all those little hang-ups already just go to prove that she would be capable of descending to the depths, the way Celine had? Celine—who had once been a normal girl, who'd held down a job, got a car, an apartment.

To his teenage eyes she'd seemed the most sophisticated woman imaginable. Beautiful, sexy, clever, and in control of all those boys with their raging hormones. They'd practically drooled over her. Of course in retrospect he could see that by knowing that above all others *he* was her choice he'd been feeding some sort of hole in his ego. Perhaps…

But all that had been before the red rages, the wild moods, the threats. Before she'd started trying to close down the rest of his life.

Just as he'd woken up to the fact that he was a fifteen-year-old boy in a relationship more straitjacketed than any marriage, she'd decided she couldn't live without him.

Oh, no. He was never, *ever* going to go through

that again. Lies. Manipulation. Guilt. Pain. Dark, dark days. Women were either fickle, governed by their emotions, or they were machines like his mother. And he didn't want any of those in his life.

So, much as he liked Lucie—and he did…he liked her a lot—he was never getting burned again.

With a start, Dante looked up. The helicopter had landed on the roof of the hotel—auto-piloted by him from somewhere out on the Hudson, it would seem.

Lucie was unclipping her belt and sticking her headphones in the pouch. The day was clear and the timing was—perfect. They had time for a quick change and then would come the start of the on-slaught. But he'd be kind. He'd be chivalrous and attentive. He'd make his mother proud and he'd make sure Lucie had a fantastic time to remember him by.

'Okay?' he asked as the doors closed on the elevator and started to drop them down to their floor.

'Dante, I'm not sure if you're aware, but that's the fourth time you've asked me that since we landed.'

He surveyed her carefully.

'And, yes, thank you very much—I am okay.'

'That's good. I'll remember that. You don't like to be asked if you're okay too often.'

'Why bother remembering? We'll be on two different continents shortly. I really don't think you need to store up any silly facts. You can be sure that *I* won't.'

She turned and stared at the coppery panels at the front of the elevator that reflected their blurred outlines. The LED display showed the floor numbers falling. And although she'd only uttered a few words Dante felt as if he'd just taken a hit to the back of the head. Interesting…

CHAPTER NINE

IF REAL ESTATE and polo failed as careers he should take up fortune-telling. Because—really—every single thing that he had predicted had come true.

His mother was *beyond* taken with Lucie. It was as if she'd prayed to the gods for a prospective daughter-in-law and, hey, one had dropped right out of the sky and into the Presidential Suite at The Park—complete with beauty, money, class and enough social graces to see her through every white tie, black tie and smart-but-casual function that could ever be dreamed up.

She had *no* idea—none—about the other stuff. Lucie's hang-ups about her body, about crowds, her hiding from the world in the middle of nowhere. The fact that she had a dysfunctional family just like almost every other person he knew. If she *did* know about it—or even suspect it—she was choosing in her own very particular way to ignore it.

And there was no way he was going to start dishing the dirt. Every single thing Lucie had told him had been in confidence. She had opened up more than he could ever have imagined—*should* ever have imagined. And that was great—but it also cast a shadow.

Trust, confidence, sharing secrets… It didn't scream *no-strings weekend* the way he'd intended. If it had been confined to trusting him with her body—which she had, becoming increasingly confident in telling him what she wanted—then, yes, she'd done that. But there was still room for more. If only he could get her away from his mother for long enough.

Eleanor had barely passed the time of day with him, but she was all over Lucie. And Lucie was being 'such a darling' back. They had 'so much in common' he'd heard—easily five times in five hours.

It was a car crash. A pile-up of all his worst dreams.

He'd never made the cut to be one of his mother's 'projects' when he'd been growing up. And his younger, needier self had at times resented the fact that she'd been there for everyone else except him. But he'd grown up fast. Too fast. And the last thing he'd wanted since Celine was any kind of simpering interference in his life. Especially from his mother—and she had happily obliged by training her lasers elsewhere.

So what she thought she was doing by monopolising Lucie through lunch and during their stroll round Central Park was anybody's guess. Except *he'd* guessed it in the first five minutes, and it wasn't cool. If she didn't let up he was going to have to take her to one side and talk to her. Firmly.

He badly wanted to have some one-on-one time
with Lucie. Whenever she came out of that damn
shower. They had two hours until showtime. Two
hours that he'd made clear were off-limits to any
member of the family who might drop by their suite
and hope for a lovely cup of English tea and a chat
about the Queen. Or whatever.

He emptied the pockets in his jeans of phone and
wallet and put his shades down on the bedside table
at his side of the bed. *His* side of the bed. What did
that even mean? *Every* side of the bed was his side.

'Hey, Princess,' he said, going up to the en-suite
bathroom door. He rapped and pushed the handle.
Locked? What was going down with her, exactly?

He lifted his hand to knock more loudly on the
door just as it swung open. A puff of steam and a
freshly scrubbed beauty emerged. Scowling.

'Hey, gorgeous,' he said, walking towards her to
grab a kiss.

'Handsome,' she said, giving him a smile and her
cheek for his kiss as she passed on into the room.

'I know you're planning to get ready, but there's
something I need to discuss with you,' he said, catching her by the waist and pulling her round to face
him. 'There's a crisis in the hotel and they need our
help.'

She was smiling at him. She *loved* these little
games they played.

'I didn't hear about any crisis. Are you quite sure
you've not got the wrong end of the stick?'

He winked. 'It's a laundry crisis. They need their towels back. *Now.*'

She squealed and tried to move out of his grasp, but he was fast and strong and totally determined.

'I'm reporting you to the management!' she cried, giggling and writhing and then sighing as she allowed herself to be held, allowed him to unknot her towel. Allowed him to unwrap her and slide his hands all over that warm, damp, glorious flesh.

'You drive me crazy,' he said, pulling her close against him, sliding her lush, beautiful body against his. He pulled the towel off her head, ran his hands through her hair and held her head, tugged her even closer. 'God, you're lovely. *Lovely.*'

He found her mouth, and just that meeting of her lips on his lips had him straining so hard again. It was like a frenzy. He couldn't get enough of her. He still hadn't had her in all the ways he wanted. He'd taken his time, gone at her pace, but now he was crazy with need. He wanted *all* of her.

'Come on, baby,' he said, filling his hands with her breasts, filling his mouth with her nipple, laving it over and over, tugging and sucking. Kneading and loving. Walking her back to the bed.

Her hands dropped to his head, holding him there at her breasts, and her moans filled the room. She was as crazy for him as he was for her.

She said his name, over and over. She moaned and cried out. And he knew she was ripe for him—ready for every last bit of pleasure he could give her. It was time. Her last taboo.

He laid her down on the bed, pink and damp, those rosy-tipped breasts so prominent, so erotic, so purely, perfectly lovely.

He stood over her.

'Touch yourself, Lucie.'

She was flat on the bed. She was writhing, lost in her own pleasure. She was ready.

'Now.'

Her eyes flew open but she did as he said. She lifted her hand and laid it between her legs. And he watched as she began to slide her fingers over her bud.

'That's it, sweetheart. That's it.'

He lay down beside her on the bed as she closed her eyes and turned her head away.

'Baby…you beautiful girl.'

Gently he cupped her jaw and turned her to face him. Her eyes were glazed. He kissed her lips, kissed down between her breasts. He palmed her full, swollen flesh and pulled a nipple into his mouth. She moaned.

He shifted position and began to trail kisses down over her stomach. He waited—expecting to feel her jerk away, expecting the freeze. But still she touched and moaned, and he could not wait any more to know her in that most intimate way.

'Sweetheart…' he breathed as he slipped right down until his lips were level with her mound. 'Let me kiss you.'

He paused, and she paused—just for that tiny moment.

'*All* of you, Lucie. All of you is beautiful. Nothing should be hidden away. I love you—all of you.'

He screwed his eyes shut and bit down on a curse. He couldn't believe what he'd just said. But he had. Just said it. *Damn*.

But he'd deal with the fallout later, if there was any, because there was no way back now. She was easily the most lovely girl he'd ever known. And she was going to let him do what he should have been able to do from that first night. It was crazy that she'd needed all that nurturing and cosseting and coaxing to get her to this point. But here she was, trusting him as no one had ever trusted him before. God, it was beautiful.

He dipped his head. He kissed her most private part. He licked. She *was* beautiful.

He growled his praise and settled himself between her legs, gripping her hips and holding her just where he wanted, where she needed him. She didn't move, didn't jerk, didn't slide away or beg him to stop.

And then he found her and lapped her. Over and over. Revelling in the knowledge that *he'd* been the one to arouse her, to make her so wet, so swollen, so ready to burst into orgasm right there in his mouth.

She felt it coming, knew it was coming, and as the chatter in her head started up she would not have it.

Would not let her silly head deny her this beautiful pleasure.

The warm, wet caress of his tongue, the sight of his head in that most erotic position, pouring his pleasure into her, the touch of his lips and the steadily building crescendo finally almost peaking— and then the break, the wonderful release.

She screamed. She heard his name rush from her lips. She gripped the sheets as his tongue pulsed again and again and again until the pleasure almost became pain and she finally begged him to stop.

He climbed up beside her and held her then in his arms. She was molten. She was replete. She was happier than she could ever have imagined. She had conquered one of her biggest hang-ups and stifled the voices that dominated her head and her life. Dante had done more for her than he would ever know.

As they lay back on the bed, he still fully dressed and she naked, wrapped in his arms, she listened to the far-off noise of the street. The bustle and buzz of New York—life in all its wonderful forms. The day was rolling on, just as it had when they had strolled around the park only an hour earlier, but it was changed for ever now.

He had given her that gift. But more than that—*so* much more than that—he had told her that he loved her. In his own way, not in a conventional way, but she knew. This wonderful man who played every-thing so cool, who'd never had a girlfriend for lon-ger than five minutes, who spent his life travelling, avoiding commitment—he'd recognised that they had something special. And she had too—of course she had. She'd never had the courage to think it, never mind say it until now. But he was braver than she—he'd said it. And the only thing they could do now was move forward. Together.

But first she had to show him what he'd done for her. She had to make love to him now. She felt as if her whole life had suddenly become clear as crystal. She slid round and raised herself up above him, straddled him and began to unfasten his buttons. He'd been looking away, but now turned to face her. And he looked strangely grave, like a fallen angel.

'Dante…' She cupped his face and kissed him. She poured all her love and thanks into her kiss. 'That was so lovely. I'm sorry I was so silly, and I'm so grateful you cared enough not to give up on me. I love every part of you too.'

She bent forward to kiss him again, but he shifted, and instead of letting her lips land on his he tucked her under his arm.

'Hey…glad you enjoyed it. Knew you would.'

She was sandwiched against his chest, with her head pinned down, listening to the slow beat of his heart. She pushed herself up.

'So that's one I owe you,' she said, getting back to unbuttoning him.

'You owe me nothing, Princess.'

He twisted out of her reach, swung his legs round and sat on the edge of the bed, facing the window.

Lucie kneeled up, placed her hands on his shoulders and bent forward to kiss his cheek. She slid her hands down between the open panels of his shirt and over the fabulous muscles of his chest. She nuzzled against his neck, absorbing his scent, scenting herself.

'Hey, look at the time!' he said, grabbing her lightly, embracing her softly. Then he stood, set her back and ruffled her still-damp hair. 'I'd better hit the shower.'

Lucie sank down on her heels and watched a flutter of tiny dust diamonds sparkle in the wake of his movement. A flood of warm afternoon sun bathed the whole room in golden honey tones that softened the heavy lacquered wood. She had stated when they'd checked in that she found the furniture dark and old-fashioned. Dante had smiled, in that way he did, and said that as long as the bed was firm he didn't have a problem with any of it.

She couldn't care less about any of that now. She barely noticed anything other than the space he'd left and the creeping chill that seeped across her bare skin.

What had just happened? Why had he turned away? Refused her? Rejected her. He had used the 'L' word—he *had*! She wasn't hearing things. And then he had *rejected* her. After saying what he'd said. After making her body sing and her heart burst.

She felt hot, fat tears of self-pity spring into her eyes and wiped them furiously with her hand. This did not make sense!

She stepped onto the carpeted floor, dragging a sheet round her shoulders, and walked to the windows. To the right was the spread of another huge brownstone building, windows in a grim grid above dreary awnings and the spikes of bare flagpoles. Below a red carpet seeped like a pool of blood to the street. To the left a sliver of darkening sky showed above the jutting edifices of a thousand faceless blocks, and in between people were swarming like ants and cars and trucks were screaming their impatience.

How could the world have tilted so awfully in those moments?

The world? *Her* world—which had been on a head-on collision course with confidence and happiness—had now been sent flying off in another direction completely. Was she really going to let herself sink back into the miserable world she'd once inhabited? Was she going to stay in hiding for ever?

So he had rejected her? Well, maybe she had read it wrong. Or maybe she should care less about what other people thought and did and more about what she was going to do next. Because in her talk with Dante's mother she had learned so much about how she could put something back into the world. She had made a start with the CCC, but there were a million charities she could patronise. And she didn't need Lady Viv to come anywhere near any of them. She was more than capable of working behind the scenes herself. And, while she wasn't exactly ready to jump up onto any podium, she did feel a lot more confident that one day she would. One day soon.

But first she had to tackle this. Head-on. She'd never had any problem confronting him before—why on earth would she start now? She paced to the door of the en-suite bathroom. She could hear the shower faintly. Before she rattled the door she should think this through. Perhaps. But her hand and her brain weren't working in tandem and she shoved it open.

The pile of clothes on the floor, the steam on every flat surface, the scent of that lemon soap he used... Her heart swelled and her throat squeezed. *Dante.*

'Hey,' he said as he tilted his face up and let the running water clear it of foam. Then he wiped his cheeks and lifted more soap. He rubbed his big hand over his big chest and under his big arm. 'Everything okay?'

As if she'd wakened from a coma, she suddenly came to.

'No, it's damned well *not* okay! And you know that perfectly well.'

He continued to soap his body—down his abdomen and further. Her eyes dropped to his penis. It was still semi-hard and stuck out. Totally uninhibited, he stroked it as he covered it in soap and let the water rush off. He turned to the side, replaced the soap in its dish, and continued to rinse his body clean.

'Is that right?' he said, shrugging slightly and putting his head back under the jet of water.

'I thought you'd made me angry that first time,

when you put your paws all over me on your boat. And then when you strolled onto my father's yacht as if I should be grateful for you sharing your air with me. But to do what you just did to me is unforgivable!'

'You orgasmed in my mouth. People in Queens heard you. And *that's* unforgivable?'

Lucie stepped forward, sliding on the wet tiles and the sheet that was bunched about her feet. She stumbled and fell slightly towards him. In a flash he spun round and reached out to help her gain her balance, but all she wanted to do was drum her hands on his chest and his arms and make him feel some of the pain she was feeling.

He held her wrists. Looked right into her face. Droplets of water coursed down his brow, his nose and his chin. He blinked his eyes clear and stared and stared. His face was fixed with a look that said absolutely nothing. *Nothing.* His blue eyes might have been made from stone for all the life they contained. She stared from one to the other and back again. Nothing.

'You know what I'm talking about,' she said.

'I know that you're a mature woman who walked into this with her eyes open.'

She twisted her face away as the tears burned their way forward.

'Walked into this? I still don't even know what *this* is! You say one thing and then you say another. What am I supposed to think?'

She tugged her arms down, trying to get out of his grasp. 'Let me go! I mean it—I don't even want to look at you.'

'Calm down, Lucie.'

His voice was dense, and as dark as the wooden furniture in the bedroom. There was no light, no life in his eyes. The more he shut down, the more she wanted to start a fire under him.

'What's *wrong* with you? Why on earth are you behaving like this?'

'You need to calm down. Do your breathing. You'll be fine.'

'Stop patronising me! Who do you think you are? You *caused* this! I was breathing perfectly normally until you weirded out on me.'

She jerked her hands more purposefully this time and he let her go. He faced her—water still coursing down his right shoulder. Droplets had gathered in his eyelashes and fell from his nose and chin. He stood like a cliff behind a waterfall. Powerful, elusive, utterly inaccessible. And *still* she wanted him.

'Dante…' she said, stepping forward, wrapping her arms around him, the way she had a hundred times in the past few days.

He didn't stop her, but he was rigid like rock. She pulled back from the warm, wet, firm body. From the care and caressing he had given her these past few days. She withdrew from the heat and the light, the joy. Her world tilted again and she reached out to grab the wall, to keep herself from falling through space.

'You told me you loved me.'

He flinched—a tiny movement but she saw it. His mouth opened and then he closed it again, dropped his head to one side. He reached behind him to turn off the shower. Grabbed a towel from the rail and passed one to her.

'I'm sorry. Heat of the moment. Didn't mean anything.'

He started to dry himself in that thoroughly male way that he had. Rubbing and patting and dragging the towel this way and that. She felt as if he was rubbing himself clear of every trace of her.

'Come on, Lucie. We got carried away. We were having a great time. We've had a great time, you and me. We don't need any drama. And we've only got hours left until we need to get on our planes. Why get heavy now? Hmm?'

He wrapped the towel around his hips and stepped forward, encircled her with his arms.

'We're going to a party! We're gonna have a good time!' he said, his grin sliding back into place.

He lifted the towel she held limply in her hand and patted her shoulders dry where they had been splashed. She stood for a moment, passive. Then she grabbed the towel and tied it around her body.

'Princess? Hey, let's finish up on a high. A few more hours and I promise you will have an amazing time. I'll make sure of it.'

Her world was still at a tilt. She could let it slide even further on its back. Or she could spin it back on its axis, all by herself.

'You don't need to make sure of anything, Dante. I'm more than capable of sorting out my own "good time".'

He nodded. Beamed a brittle bright smile. 'That's more like it,' he said.

She stared at him, more and more incredulous with each passing second.

'For the record, the only reason I'm hanging on is because I made a commitment. I said I would do this and I stand by my word. I'm not some fake commitment-phobe, scared to put my money where my mouth is. I don't pretend to be someone I'm not, stifling my feelings and then lying about it.'

She couldn't quite believe that the words had been in her head, never mind that they had left her mouth. Her hand flew there, as if to slam the gate after the horse had bolted.

He had walked out of the bathroom. The door was open and his footsteps left a wet imprint on the carpet. A few droplets that had escaped his thorough towel-drying still clung like glass beads to his shoulders and in the spikes of his hair. Frozen in a shaft of late-afternoon sun, there was a haze of dust all around them, and the sense of a storm brewing was so profound she stood waiting.

'I told you to calm down, Lucie. And I meant it.'

'Calm down? What the hell are you talking about?

I don't have any *reason* to calm down. What the hell does my calming down have to do with anything?'

'You don't know what you're saying. I don't respond well to emotional blackmail, and I'm not going to be around to pick up the pieces.'

'Pieces? There are *pieces*? I just called you out. *You're* the one with the problem! You're a commitment-phobe and you're trying to turn this into something that's about *me*.' She grabbed a robe from the hook in the bathroom and shoved her arms in, tying it so tightly it hurt.

Dante moved through the room, still at that slow and steady pace, but poised as a boxer. She could feel the waves of tension. But she couldn't seem to stop herself.

'Are you still going to deny it, Dante? To me? Or—what's worse—to yourself. This has nothing to do with me going to pieces. When have you ever been close to anything that's fallen to pieces? You don't hang around long enough to see the sun set! You rock up and ship out! I'll bet you barely stay long enough to learn their names!'

'That's enough!'

He turned. A quarter-turn, but it was swift and it made her halt. And go quiet.

'You think I should learn *names*? There's only one name in my head. As if it's carved into my skull. And until I rub it out there will be no one else. Do you hear me, Lucie? Not you. Not anyone else. I don't want to be responsible for anyone else again. *Ever.*'

Lucie stood, her hand on the robe's soft towelling belt, her fingers slipping over the knot she had tied, unable to loosen it.

'You've no idea about my past—what I went through.'

'What you went through...? Poor Dante. Did someone hurt you?' She stepped forward. 'You think you're the only one who's ever been hurt? I've been around hurt. I propped up my mother after my father left her. I saw her pain. And she got through it. So it doesn't add up that you're going to lock down your emotions and check out of life because of a little bit of hurt.'

She tugged and tugged at the stupid belt and eventually it came loose. She glanced to the side, where the dress she was planning to wear to the awards dinner was hanging like some ghoulish spectre, observing them. Dante moved to his bag, pulled out underwear, shook off the towel and started to get dressed.

He had his back to her. She knew he was listening, but it was as if he was putting more and more distance between them. As if he had rubbed her off his skin in the shower and was now rubbing her out of his mind.

'Why can't you answer me? Why can't you tell me even one single thing about this—this woman? Help me understand why you're acting like this?'

'You're really not going to give up, are you?'

'Not if it's going to help me understand what's

going on in your head, Dante. Not if there's a chance that this weekend might have a different outcome.'

'There's only one outcome, Lucie. And it hasn't changed since I drew up the terms on my yacht.'

'Is that all love is to you, Dante? A business deal?'

'You really want to know what love is to me? The last woman I loved took her own life. Because I wouldn't do what she wanted me to do. Is *that* a big enough detail for you? Does that help? Will you leave it alone now?'

CHAPTER TEN

LIKE A SEA of giant white polka dots, tables extended into the farthest corners of the hotel's grand ballroom. A wall of silver curtains encircled them, and to the front, accessed by a short sweep of steps on either side, was the imposing empty stage. A single spotlight splashed harsh yellow light down onto a solitary lectern, from which poked a long, thin microphone, and a vast screen articulated clearly that this was indeed the Twenty-fifth Annual Woman of the Year Awards.

As guests in silks and satins, jewel-bright, and in black and white took their seats, waiters hovered and then swept round them, brandishing bottles and laying out plates with a flourish. Glasses seemed to be permanently fizzing and popping, and the buzz of conversation tinkled higher and louder with each passing minute.

The heavy leaden twist of Lucie's stomach had not eased in the two hours since Dante had uttered his declaration about his first love and then silently finished dressing. She had known that her overwhelming instinct—to go to him, hold him, comfort him—would be completely rejected. Instead they'd both skirted each other in some choreographed dance, as if it was a thousand years and the vast dry sands of the Sahara that lay between them rather than an opalescent wool carpet and a half-hour deadline.

She'd watched from the corners of her eyes, aching for him, but he hadn't acknowledged her pleas and within moments had been dressed, and back in the easy, lazy zone he commanded so well.

With a curt, 'Back in ten,' he'd left her sitting at the dressing table, a clutter of products in front of her. *Miracle* this and *Illusion* that. She'd picked up one of the tiny tubes and bottles, refusing to believe that what they had shared had been an illusion. She'd travelled so far from the person she'd been that no matter what happened she would always treasure this time. But it was painful to think that for Dante it had been just another few days...

She'd shuddered. She wasn't judging. He'd clearly been through hell. And to live with the pain of feeling responsible for someone else's decision to end their life was unimaginable. She had seen her mother in agonies of despair, had brought her handkerchiefs in her childish way, trying to make her feel better, but this was something entirely different. No wonder Dante wanted nothing to do with love.

He'd returned, wordlessly, as she'd clipped her earrings into place. She'd glanced at him in the mirror but that rocky edifice had still been intact. If she had known what to say it might have helped, but she hadn't, and they had noiselessly finished getting ready and then joined his family—straight from the arctic silence of their room to the warm, excited hubbub of aperitifs and air-kisses.

Lucie glanced across the table to where Dante now sat, his body tilted slightly to the side, engaged in conversation with his sister-in-law, Frankie. He was at his most handsome, in black tails, white bow tie and sharp-collared shirt. His golden skin and dark blond hair were utterly arresting. He stopped her heart—it was that simple.

Inwardly stifling the pain of another stab of hurt at how their time together was trickling to its close, Lucie allowed her glass to be refilled and stole another glance across the table, watching as he nodded slowly, occasionally allowing a dimple to form, as he reacted to Frankie's ebullient delivery of some story or other involving polo ponies and a great deal of hand gestures.

Frankie looked so radiantly, contentedly happy. Her skin glowed with the hormones of the early pregnancy she and Rocco had announced when she'd beamingly refused the first of the glasses of champagne that had been passed around. Rocco had put his arms around her, laid his chin on her head and squeezed his eyes shut as if he couldn't give enough thanks to God for her very existence.

At that moment Lucie had glanced at Dante. He had looked cast in stone, immobile, but had only stayed like that for mere seconds before he'd slipped on the full-power, two-dimpled smile and twinkling eyes charm mask. He'd slapped his brother's back affectionately, shaken his hand, embraced Frankie gently and convinced the whole gathering that he'd never heard happier news.

Only Lucie knew differently.

She could see past the golden glow, the sunburst smiles and the azure-blue eyes, and with every passing moment it was clearer and clearer to her that Dante simply wasn't able to form *any* kind of relationship that would lead to commitment—never mind a wedding or children.

So her mother had been right after all. Playboy. Heartbreaker. Just like her father. A boy in a man's body. Never wanting to grow up, never wanting to take on responsibility. Wanting a lifetime of playing the field.

Right on cue a striking-looking brunette appeared behind him. She placed her hands over his eyes and leaned in close. 'Surprise!' she whispered in a sultry voice, and as he turned to see who it was she twisted herself *and* her full cleavage almost into his face.

'Lana! How lovely to see you.' Dante composed himself and stood up. He kissed each proffered cheek, holding her at a distance that was *just* acceptable.

'Mind if borrow your date?' the brunette threw at Lucie as she slid her arm through Dante's, without waiting for a reply, and walked with him to another table.

'Subtle, huh?' said a voice at her side. Frankie. 'You get used to it. In time. I spent the first six months ready to claw their eyes out, you know?'

Lucie dragged her gaze back from where Dante was being pawed and stroked to the quirky smiling face of Dante's sister-in-law.

'Every time I was taken to a function like this I'd ask Rocco for a pre-match report—you know, to prepare for former lovers launching themselves at him. And then I'd stick to him the whole night, scanning the joint and making it obvious he was with me and me alone.'

'Sounds like a lot of work,' said Lucie, her eyes darting back to where Dante was now meeting and greeting the rest of the table.

'Oh, it was, yes. I stopped as soon as I realised that Rocco might be the most handsome man in the world, as far as I was concerned, but he was also the most loyal. He could see past every one of those offers he was getting. What's a roll in the hay compared to a lifetime of happiness? As soon as I accepted that I stopped trying to beat everyone off with a stick.'

'Yes, well, perhaps there's more than just hair colour that separates the brothers,' said Lucie, rather archly. 'Sorry,' she added, when Frankie's elfin features knitted into a frown. 'It's not that I don't applaud your efforts. But I'm just passing through.'

'Dante's worth the effort. *More* than worth it. Everything good in life is. You get back what you put

in. I'm not saying it's about being on your guard—
I'm saying it's about understanding one another...
accepting one another.'

Lucie nodded. She smiled. 'And *I'm* saying that
the first step is accepting yourself. I've just turned
that corner. And he helped me to do that.'

'I can imagine.' Frankie sat back in her chair. Her
hands fell to her tiny bump. 'He's a good man,' she
said. 'The best.'

Lucie looked across at him. At the man she loved.
She loved. The man who would not admit that he
loved her back.

Time was running out for her to do anything. Another few hours here, for the ceremony itself, then
dancing, and then—that was it. Curtains closed.
Back to their room and then goodbye.

A rumble of anticipation went around the room,
signalling that the awards were about to be announced. Dante excused himself and came back to
their table.

The house lights and stage lights dimmed until
only the glow from hundreds of flickering candles lit
the cavernous space. Suddenly an uplifting overture
boomed through the speakers and the Master of Cer-
emonies walked out onto the stage. The huge screen
started to show images of the ballroom, focusing in
on various tables and various dignitaries and celebri-
ties. Whoops and applause followed when the camera
hit upon someone of particular interest to the crowd.

There was no doubt that the women here were

massively important figures in their worlds, be it literature, fashion, art, medicine, acting, science, business, community or politics.

A voice boomed out that these pictures were being beamed live around the world, and then there on the giant screen was their table. The voice, which it soon became apparent belonged to a roving reporter, told the ballroom—and presumably the world—that here was Eleanor Hermida and her family. They heard that she was due to be honoured shortly and that her wonderful family were here to share her joy. And wasn't that Lady Vivienne Bond's daughter there with them?

Lucie's heart leaped into her mouth. Of course she'd known there would be cameras, that it was a live broadcast. But nothing intrusive—nothing that involved any attention on *her*. That wasn't part of the deal! She was here as a date, as an icon of her own free will that her mother could observe from wherever she was on the planet. Free will that declared her independence.

The last thing—the *very* last thing—she wanted the world or her mother to see was her fumbling for words or breath. Thankfully the camera zoomed off to another table. She sat back in her seat and expelled a huge lungful of air through clenched teeth. She *had* to get this under control. It was a dinner—nothing else. She was a guest at a dinner, just as hundreds of others were.

'Everything all right?' Dante leaned across.

For the first time since they'd entered the ball-room his gaze snapped straight onto hers, and in that second a thousand things fell into place. Whatever he was looking for in this world, a simpering, vacuous woman wasn't it.

Lucie straightened her spine, tugged her shoulders back, raised her chin and thanked God and her mother's incessant moaning for at least this default face-saving movement.

'Of course,' she chimed. 'Isn't it wonderful? I feel honoured to be here. All these worthy women, doing such worthwhile things for their causes.'

The swell of applause caused both of them to turn back to face the podium. The moment had come to honour Eleanor. A reverent hush spread round the room. A montage of pictures of some of the projects she had supported began to roll on the screen and a quick summary of her achievements sounded out.

The lights dimmed further, apart from the single yellow spot that illuminated her, and the room was imbued with humbled silence. The Master of Cere-monies relayed tales of her years of work, the money she'd raised, the lives she'd touched. And then, in a poignant tribute, a young man who'd benefited took to the stage to deliver a speech and present the life-time award.

Eleanor sat completely composed.

Well, that's where he gets it, thought Lucie. Not a flicker of emotion other than a smile more enig-matic than the Mona Lisa's. Not a hint or a suggestion that anything other than supreme self-possession ran through her veins, like liquid steel through iron pipes.

She looked at Dante and Rocco. Nothing. Complete control. Frankie was weeping, but that could be explained by her hormones—and anyway she was a Hermida only by marriage. But as Lucie looked around she saw other people similarly moved. She saw handkerchiefs pressed to eyes, heads shaking in disbelief. This woman was exceptional. Her achievements unsurpassed. But she and her sons looked as if they were listening to a travel report.

Even when Eleanor took to the podium herself, to deliver her acceptance speech, in which she paid homage to the patience of her family, their masks remained intact—Rocco's dark stare and Dante's golden gaze. Immovable. Solid. Set.

What hope did she have of piercing his impenetrable shield? He had no wish, no desire to let anyone chip through the rock to see what happiness there might be underneath. He was made of something other than flesh and blood. He had given her so much—had helped her past her own terrors, made her at home in her own skin—yet he wasn't prepared to step out from the golden shield he hid behind—his mask.

Eleanor returned to the table. Her boys kissed her courteously and saw her seated. Frankie beamed and Lucie watched, spellbound. The understated grace was mesmeric, the filial attention hypnotic. The only thing missing was any genuine warmth. And the lack of that, as far as Lucie was concerned, was the most emotional aspect of all.

A standing ovation marked the end of the awards and the start of the dancing. People left their tables and started milling around, and Lucie felt her anxiety surge. She had convinced herself that she would be able to deal with strangers with Dante by her side, but now…? After all the emotion of earlier…? Now she'd rather just slope off to the bathroom and wait it out. No one would really notice if she took a very long time to powder her nose.

She lifted her clutch and started to make her way through the people. The music had changed and a deep, heavy bass was drawing people onto the floor. She noticed Rocco and Frankie, clasped in a slow dance, but though she looked all around there was no sign of Dante. The floor continued to fill. Her need to get some air continued to build. She could see the archway that led to the restrooms and she put her head down.

And there in her way was a tall, blond, handsome figure in full white tie. Dante—with his back to her.

And then he turned. Draped around him was the slim brunette. Her backless dress was scooped so low that Lucie could almost see the cheeks of her bottom—but not quite, because Dante's hands were resting there. And as they swayed to the music the brunette tipped back her head and laughed.

Lucie looked to see the flash of white teeth, the

burst of flame-blue eyes, the shock of blond hair. Two proud dimples.

They swayed to the music, the brunette pressing herself close as they moved. He spoke…she laughed again…and Lucie saw exactly what Frankie had meant. This was it for him. This was how he lived. This was what women did to him. All the time. Just as with her father, they threw themselves at him. It was his version of love.

He'd had his fingers burned with love in his youth and had learned that it was much easier to play the super-shallow, super-smooth playboy. Just as her mother had said.

Frankie could say all she wanted about him being worth the fight, but what price lay ahead? Couldn't he even see out the end of this evening before he defaulted back to Dante the Lothario?

Anger bloomed inside her.

She put her head down and pushed past them.

She saw feet, heard voices, the pulsing bass of the music and the high, happy calls of people celebrating. The archway was close, and she brushed past a waiter pushing a trolley piled high with rows and towers of chalky-coloured *petits-fours*.

'Lucie.'

It was his voice. Deep and commanding. She ignored it.

'Hey, what do you think you're doing?'

The waiter stopped his trolley as she felt her arm pulled back and heard Dante's voice hissing in her ear.

She spun round to face him. 'Get your hands off me! Don't ever touch me again!' she hissed.

He grabbed her by the hand and put his arm around her so quickly that in seconds he had steered her down a harshly lit, plushly carpeted corridor. Her heels sank and snagged as she walked. And then he stopped, turned and twisted her round.

'Get off!' she spat, tugging out of his grip.

'Do not speak to me like that.'

'Like what? You deserve it.'

'For what? Dancing?'

'I couldn't give a damn if you dance with an entire troupe of naked go-go dancers—but not tonight! Not when you invited me here as your partner. Even though you've spent the past five hours making it perfectly clear to me *and* everyone else that that's the last thing I am!'

'It was only a dance. I *know* her. She's an old friend, for God's sake.'

'It looked to me as if you'd like to get to know her a whole lot better. Your hands were all over her backside. Is that it, Dante? Have you spent too long with just one woman? Did it all get a bit stale after—what?—five days? Are you reminding yourself what its like to have your pick? Just to reassure yourself that your commitment phobia is absolutely the right thing to have?'

For a moment it was as if a torch had been lit behind his eyes. For a moment she saw through the glare to the man. Anger. Passion. His eyes were like bright blue flames. Fire inside. And then as quickly it was doused.

'I was having a dance with an old friend. And you made a fool of yourself.'

'Yes, I did, didn't I? By agreeing to this stupid charade. But there's no point crying about it. We've only got a few hours left, and then we can chalk this one up to a very bad experience.'

'You don't mean that. We had a great time.'

'*Had* a great time. *Had.* Until you turned out to be a deluded liar. Now, get out of my way.'

She pushed past him. The corridor stretched ahead. Candelabra stuck out like wizened brass claws, grasping into the empty air. Ugly oil paintings of pastoral scenes in hugely ornate frames studded each wall. A little girl in a wide skirted dress with a satin bandeau ran past her, chased by another, laughing and screaming.

'Lucie!'

'Go to hell,' she said to the stagnant breeze.

Too angry for tears, she kept her head high and her chest out. She passed by the bathrooms. Too late now to hide out. She made her mind up to go on. The hateful crowd and the throbbing music were drawing her like some hideous harpies, luring her to the rocks.

The ballroom itself was thronged with people, slowed by the seven-course dinner and made noisy by wine. She paused for a second, to locate Eleanor and the others. She had to say her goodbyes. It was the least she could do. And then she could simply leave. It would be that easy. Leave and grieve and get on with her life.

'Lady Lucinda—how lovely to see you here in New York. And with the Woman of the Year Lifetime Achievement recipient herself! May we ask how you are connected?'

Lucie stared into the overly made up face of a reporter who had materialised from thin air. She could see thick lines of kohl eyeliner drawn around each slightly wrinkled eye, every mascaraed spike of her eyelashes, the slight smudge of her lipstick where it had bled past her mouth. She saw the scratchy black head of the microphone that had been thrust under her nose and the camera that sat on some man's shoulder.

'I…I…'

She stepped back, suddenly aware of the aeons of time and space that were opening up all around her as the woman waited for her to finish the sentence. She could sense a wave of movement as people close by turned their heads to watch, and she tried again to speak. But the voices had started in her head. Chattering on in their infernal way, telling her that she wouldn't be able to answer, that she would let her mother down and her father down. And now, to add to it all, Eleanor Hermida, who radiated such composure, would know that silly, ungainly Lucinda Bond couldn't even answer a simple question.

Her legs began to shake and her heart raced, and a sickening black fog suddenly began to fall all around her. The sea of people became a yawning pit of faces, greedy for her failure. She felt vomit rise.

And then she felt him.

Dante's arm was upon her shoulders and he pulled her to his side. He held her cold, clammy hand in his, and then there was his voice in her ear, telling her to breathe. She did. She breathed. And she felt him nuzzle the side of her face, felt his lips on her cheek.

Fear trumped anger—but love trumped fear.

She let him.

'Well, that answers one question!' said the reporter as she beamed a smile right into the camera. 'I guess you're here to give respect to Eleanor Hermida? You've heard for yourself of her many accomplishments this evening. What do you want to add for the people back home?'

Lucie lifted her chin and smiled. Those spiky mascaraed eyes were still blinking at her, but the reporter's face was beaming in an expectant smile. She felt the air pass through her nose, her throat. In and out slowly. She felt her mouth opening. She looked into the square black box of the camera.

'She's a wonderful woman,' she said.

It wasn't exactly the Declaration of Independence, but for Lucie it was the speech of her life.

The reporter nodded enthusiastically and then whooped off with her crew to another group. Lucie stood, stunned. Her heart pounded in her ears and her cheeks burned like firebrands. The mental chatter started up again in her head, but this time it was cheering her on. She had done it. She had actually overcome the sickness and formed a sentence in front of strangers. In front of the world. She had found her voice.

She turned to look at Dante. He had helped her. He had given her that little push of confidence, shown that bit of faith—all she needed—but she had done it herself.

But no amount of well-timed pecks on the cheek could erase what he had done to her this evening.

'Thanks,' she said. And turned to walk away.

'Lucie, wait,' he said. 'I owe you an apology.'

She stopped in her tracks, waited until he came level with her.

'We owe each other nothing. Remember?'

CHAPTER ELEVEN

THE COPPER-PLATED ELEVATOR moved at a sedate pace. Lucie stared at their silent shimmery reflections. The doors opened into their suite, lit lamps glowed. Lucie walked in ahead of him—ten steps across parquet, three steps down on silk-carpeted stairs. She longed to rip the heeled shoes from her feet and hurl them in the bin, to get out of the dress, the underwired bra and the Brazilian thong and throw open the window and launch them into the night air. She longed to be free of this whole experience.

'I hope your mother enjoyed her evening,' she said instead. 'Despite your glacial mood.'

'It was a sham, and you know it. The whole thing. End to end.' He walked on through the lounge, unfastened his cufflinks—one then the other—his words as wooden as the floor.

'So now it's your mother's fault you're in this awful mood?'

He sat on the bed heavily, as if he really was made of rock. Shoes came off, tie was flipped open, pulled off and cast aside. Shirt swiftly unbuttoned. He stood then. Faced her. Peeled it off. And there he was in all his pure male form, and her eyes burned with the image.

'My relationship with my mother is not up for discussion.'

'Perhaps not. But your relationship with me is.'

He almost flinched when she said the word 'relationship'. His eyes squeezed shut, just for a second, but there was no mistaking it.

'I owe you an apology and I meant it. I should never have asked you to do this. It was naïve of me to think that you and I could pull this off without someone reading more into it than there is.'

'"Someone" meaning me?'

'I thought I was clear, Lucie. I tried to be clear that this was only a short-term affair. I said at the start that there would be no happy-ever-after.'

'Yes, you were honest. At the start. But things changed, Dante. I know they did. For both of us.'

He looked at her, but there was no light, no life in his eyes—as if there was no audience to play to any more. She'd never seen him like this. Never seen him so closed down. The contrast between *her* Dante and this was unbearable. She couldn't comprehend it.

'What are you going to say next, Dante? That none of those things happened? That you didn't say you loved me? Of all the things I pegged you for, being a liar wasn't one of them!'

He stared at her. And she saw it again—she'd penetrated his mask. His eyes were lit up and his mouth was a thin, angry line.

'Good try, Princess. But it isn't going to work. I learned a long time ago not to take the bait.'

'Why do you think everything is a game? I'm not baiting you! I've had it now. All I want is to understand *why* you did what you did. Why you spent all that time…'

Her voice trailed off as she furiously bit down on the giant sob that had risen like a fist into her throat.

'Why you spent all that time loving me. Because that's what you did, Dante. You made love to me.'

He unfastened the strap of his watch—his grandfather's watch. The one he'd been wearing when he'd hauled her onto his speedboat. The minute they'd got to the Hamptons he'd had it picked up and repaired. For a moment she recalled the joy in his face when he'd got it back—real joy.

He slid it off and cradled it in his hand, then walked to the bedside table and laid it down gently, lovingly. And in that single motion she saw a flicker of something—something worth saving. Something worth all the effort in the world.

She paced towards him, arms out, imploring.

'Maybe if you explained what happened? Maybe if you opened up about it?'

'Opened up about *what*? I'm not the guy you want me to be. That's it.'

'You know what I'm talking about, Dante. You're capable of love but you've made up your mind that you don't want it because of whatever it was that happened all those years ago.'

'Whatever it was? I was a fifteen-year-old, having a love affair with a woman twice my age. If you could call it that. Miss di Rosso. She was supposed to teach us *science*.' He scoffed woodenly at the word. 'Taught me plenty of other stuff. Is that what you want to hear? Are you shocked, Lucie?'

He looked right at her now.

'You in all your first-time innocence.'

'I'm not so innocent now. Why don't you let me in? I could help, Dante—I'm sure I could.'

But he just shook his head, as if she was a memory herself—a fading figment of his imagination.

'Celine di Rosso...' He lifted his grandfather's watch. 'I would have done anything for her. Anything she wanted. I stole this watch.' He lifted it up, showed it to her from across the room. 'From my own grandfather. She wanted nice things, good times. She thought I had money. Of my own. I stole this to sell it, to pay for us to have sordid sex in a sordid motel out of town.'

Lucie watched, mesmerised. His face shifted from glazed and expressionless to anger, revulsion.

'I pawned my grandfather's watch so that I could take that woman to a sleazy dump and have sex with her because that was what she wanted. And what Celine wanted, Celine got. Every time.'

'But she was your *teacher*, Dante. You weren't old enough to know what was going on—she was abusing you!'

He made a face, replaced the watch on the bedside table and stared down at it.

'And I let her. We all have choices. I was old enough to know what I was getting myself into. I just wasn't smart enough to know how to get myself back out.'

'But surely she was terrified that someone would find out? Surely she saw it was going to end in disaster?'

'Terrified? She wasn't afraid of anything. She was a manipulative, crazy bitch. She wanted control—in everything. Where we went. When. What we did. What gifts she was to get. And when I started to wake up—when I began to call time on her demands— that's when things started to get really heavy.'

He looked round the room, as if seeking some sort of distraction.

'Anyway, you don't want to know this stuff. It's all in the past.'

'But it's haunting your present.'

A jug of water stood on a sideboard between two lamps. Four crystal tumblers and a small silver ice bucket. A tiny bowl of sliced fresh lemon. She followed his gaze as he walked over and began to pour himself a glass of water. Carefully he picked up the tongs, opened the ice bucket and dropped in three cubes. He swilled the glass, stared at it.

'It's all in the past,' he said again, his voice hollow.

'That woman did you a disservice, Dante. She was

in a position of trust and she abused that trust. And now you have a terrible view of all women because of that. She was unstable.'

He swallowed the water, drained the glass, placed it on the table.

'She blew my mind—and then she blew her own. Called me on the phone while she did it. I heard the gun. I was on my way to see her at the boathouse where we would meet. I was going to tell her it was over. She beat me to it.'

Lucie felt her hand fly to her mouth. 'Oh, my God. I'm so sorry.'

'That's when I really learned the meaning of the phrase "emotional blackmail". It doesn't get more emotional than that.'

He picked up the glass and tipped the ice cubes into his mouth, crunched them.

'I don't know what to say.'

'There's nothing to say. It happened. Life moves on.'

'But not yours. Your life is stuck. Normal people don't act like that. She seduced a boy half her age and then—then killed herself. It's possible you have such a jaded view of women because you went through all that.'

'Don't psychoanalyse me, Lucie. I've spent years going over what happened—I don't need your ten-second therapy.'

Hot sharp tears sprang to her eyes. He walked back over to the bedside, oblivious.

'I'm not psychoanalysing you. I'm only trying to understand you.'

He pulled his phone from his pocket and stood staring at it, each broad groove and cleft of muscle and bone in his chest and shoulders in light and shade from the lamps. Lucie could feel her fists bunching in the watery satin of her dress, could feel the world she'd thought she'd found slipping away as the ravine between them yawned into a gaping gorge. Soon there would be no way back.

'What time do you want to go to the airport? I don't think joining the family for breakfast is the best idea.'

She had to try one more time.

'Dante—you did more for me than anyone has ever done. You helped me—you *rescued* me! You showed me things and *mended* me and...'

Tears oozed from her eyes. She wiped them furiously.

'You told me loved me, Dante.'

Her voice closed over those last words—words that were her lifeline. She had thrown it out and all she could do now was watch to see if he would catch it.

Still and silent he stood. As perfect a figure of a man as it was possible to imagine. But only so much of him was flesh and blood. He was a man whose heart was stone.

She felt the tracks of her tears as they streaked down her face. She felt the painful lump form in her throat. She tried to swallow as the entire room slipped into a series of glazed shapes. She longed for him to come to her, to hold her, cradle her.

'I'm sorry, Lucie. It should never have happened.'

He walked into the bathroom.

And closed the door.

In the silence of the room candles flickered skittishly, mockingly doubled in each mirror's glare. Each flame a tiny glassy yellow flicker, dancing in the dim light.

There was the dull sound of the shower... The deadened hubbub of the never sleeping streets... The sounds of life starting up again...

She had done what she could. She had truly tried to make him see. But he was locked in his own glass coffin, frozen in time, living a life with the guarantee of never being hurt again. Because how could he be hurt if he kept his heart buried away?

He would have his fun—he would have his parties and his women. And in time when she heard his name she might remember him fondly. But right now she had to put as much distance and time between them as she could. She had to get herself away from the sight of him, the scent of him, the *sense* of him.

She couldn't see that body one more time and know she would never feel those arms around her, never lay her face against his smooth firm chest... Never hear her name from his lips...the way he rolled the 'L'...the way he smiled when he said 'Princess'...

To know that those moments of wakening together, when he'd gather her into his arms, press himself into her back, slip inside her...to know that it would never happen again.

Tears coursed freely down her face. She saw nothing but images of Dante. Facing her open-mouthed on his speedboat, mocking her as he stood between the turtle posters, beaming with two dimples and lifting her, spinning her in the air at Little Hauk. Walking along the beach.

Huge, silent sobs racked her body as the shower continued to flow.

She wiped her hands across her eyes, her nose and cheeks. She gathered up her bag and her passport. Her phone.

She looked around to see the debris of their day, but it was too painful now. She couldn't bear to see their shared things, his things she'd never see again.

She crossed the opalescent carpet, moved up the three steps and onto the landing. Back across the parquet floor. She pressed the button and waited for the copper-tinted elevator.

Two steps in, she turned. The doors closed. Her own image, alone, was the reflection now.

In the suite the bathroom door opened. Steam bled into the empty space.

CHAPTER TWELVE

IT WAS HARD to be sure when he'd begun to feel anything again. Hard to know when the mist had cleared enough for him to see that what other people were telling him. That he'd changed. That he'd lost his 'sparkle'—whatever that was. That he'd become harder, fiercer, angrier.

All of that was true. He made no apology for any of it. The alternative didn't bear thinking about— give in, give up, let the team down? Let Marco down? He needed a series of wins in Dubai to make him rock-solid as a commodity. He was going all out for every investment opportunity available. He knew that the Hermanos Hermida brand was his now. And just because his heart had been ripped out of his body, it didn't mean that he should inflict that pain on anyone else.

There was always a bright side. Always. In the middle of utter blackness he knew there was. He couldn't see it. Had no idea when he *would* see it. But it was a certainty that it would come.

'This time will pass,' his grandfather had used to say. Even on the day when he'd called him to his study and asked what had happened to his watch. Even when Dante had silently refused to tell him why he had pawned it—not in fear, but in dread of how ashamed he would make the old man feel.

It hadn't worked, though. He had given him the money to get the watch back. Money that Dante had paid back by working every hour that God sent—labouring in the city, far enough away so that no one knew who he was.

The timing had been perfect. Just when he'd needed something to bury himself in, had needed to work until his muscles ached, using his body heaving hard materials and risking his own life on high-rise building sites because that was what he deserved. Celine had died. And he had slipped back into his adolescent world, realising that he was just another privileged pupil in one of her classes.

He'd spent days waiting for the police to come. Days until he'd given up and gone to them himself. They told him to 'run along'. He knew his grandfather had had a hand in it. But it had never been mentioned. Not a whisper, not a look, not an embrace. There had been nothing to suggest that anyone had any idea that Miss di Rosso had been any more to Dante than the teacher who'd once taught him.

This time will pass. And it had. Days had bled into weeks, into months and years. Until it had taken an actual *doppelgänger* to make him remember her at all.

This time… This pain… The days had bled as his heart had bled. But there was no let-up, no sign of a clot forming, let alone a scar. No sign that this time would ever pass. The bright side was that he could still put one foot in front of the other. That he could still ride a horse and fire a ball past three players. That he could raise money and invest money and had put the Little Hauk Polo Foundation on the map. And he had. He had cleaned up. He was on fire. He was 'the man to watch'. 'Unstoppable'.

Everyone's hero.

He stepped out from the club house now. As was his routine. It was all about routines now. The little things that were part of his day—to make sure that the wheels of his life kept turning. Like running on the beach—the beach she'd declared her favourite. Like eating at the breakfast table and ignoring the image of her that sprang to mind and would choke him if he let it. Because she was everywhere. In everything.

What a fool! *What a fool.* He'd thought it was Lucie who had fallen hard! He'd been worried that she had cast her dream net wide and tried to ensnare him in a life of picket fences and *Hi, honey, I'm home.* He'd been so busy worrying about her projections that he'd never noticed for a second that he'd fallen deeply in love himself. He'd been so de-

termined to make sure she'd take a different fork in
the road that he hadn't seen the edge of the cliff and
had run right off it himself.

'Hey! Handsome!'

He turned at the sound of Marco's voice. Even
those words pierced through his heart for a moment,
as if he'd just stepped out of the bathroom at The
Park and into the sickening vacuum that his life had
become since that moment he'd found her gone.

'S'up?' he called back, slowing his pace to let his
buddy catch up.

His buddy with whom he'd shared everything—
apart from any discussion about Celine. And now
Lucie.

'I'm heading to Betty's. Wanna come?'

'No, thanks. I've got a ton of stuff to do here tonight.'

They walked along in the early-evening sunshine,
strides matching, shadows lengthening before them.

'Ah, yeah, of course. Those blades of grass won't
count themselves.'

Dante paused, turned to look at Marco, who had
continued to walk on.

'What's that supposed to mean?'

Marco shrugged, looked back at him.

'Well, it's the sort of out-of-character irrelevant
nonsense you seem to be dedicating your life to. Instead of moving on, forgetting about her. There are
loads of fish in that sea,' he said, casting his arm out

in a wide sweep. 'Come on, you're not trying to tell me she's "the one"?'

Dante stared at him, trying to follow what he was saying.

'I mean, yeah, she was pretty—but not amazing. And she had a good body... Okay, she had a great body—and that rack—but she wasn't—'

Dante didn't know what had happened until it happened, and he saw his best friend staring at him with dazed eyes, clutching the side of his face where he'd just taken a punch. Blue and purple bloomed under his hand and a trickle of blood escaped from the corner of his mouth. Dante's fist ached, and he looked at the red mark that now formed there.

'Hell, there's nothing much wrong with your uppercut, is there?'

'What did you say that for? What are you trying to say about her? You aren't fit to breathe the same air as her, you piece of crap.'

'Well, that makes two of us,' Marco said through lips that seemed to be swelling. 'Because you're as much fun as a hot date with death. She'll have moved on by now anyway. Why would she hang around waiting on a loser like you if she's that great?'

Dante swung again, but this time Marco blocked him. They struggled together, pushing against one another, heels kicking up the dust of the day. The ponies moved warily closer, then edged away.

'You got me once but you won't get me again,'

Marco hissed. 'Why don't you take all that energy and redirect it to getting her back. Give us all a break. God knows we need it—we've been looking at your moping face for months now. You're putting me off my chowder and the damn horses off their game.'

Dante gave him a final shove and fell back against the fence. His friend's comments had taken the wind from him and he stepped to the side, leaned his two hands against the warm, smooth wood and hung his head.

'It's that obvious?'

'Of *course* it's obvious! From the moment you took her to Betty's we could all see that you were perfect for one another. But you and your crazy rules about women—you never gave it a chance.'

Dante stared across the fields. He had created this place in six months flat. Training ground, stables, clubhouse and gym. He had worked round the clock and poured every last ounce of energy into making it perfect. He had shut himself off from everything, making this the excuse, when all the while he'd known—and clearly so did everyone else—that he was hiding out, licking his wounds.

Well, no more.

'Hey, where are you going?' Marco's voice trailed into his back.

'To get back in the game. To get on with my life. To get my woman.'

'I'd get yourself some kevlar first, buddy. Or a

suit of armour. I don't think she's going to just roll over for you.'

Dante dusted his hands together. He stared out across the yard. The sun was fiery and sinking fast. There were about a million chores to be done before he hit the sack. But all of it could wait. There was nothing more important than this.

'This really is the most spectacular view of the bay,' said Lady Vivienne, lowering her tiny white binoculars, squinting at the scene and then raising them again. 'What a lot of fabulous yachts. One could quite easily stay here all day and not become bored.'

Lucie replaced her cup in its saucer, where it rested on her knee. She looked to where her mother was pointing, registering that there were indeed a lot more gleaming white yachts in the bay than even an hour ago.

'Do you think they're all here for Simon's wedding?'

A swell of something close to nausea threatened to burst into her throat, but Lucie was well prepared now, and immediately wiggled her toes and tuned in her attention. It was remarkable just how easily she was able to control those impulses now. They still happened—they probably always would—but the dedicated sessions she'd had with a psychologist meant she was much more in control now. Thank heavens.

'I think there's every chance, Mother. You have invited nearly everyone in possession of a yacht, after all.'

'Not *everyone*,' her mother replied archly. 'Your father, for one. And that awful—'

'That's enough!' said Lucie sharply, before her mother could say another word. She placed the cup and saucer on the breakfast table and stood up, slowly and deliberately dusting the crumbs from her linen dress. She had only been sitting on the balcony of this Majorcan cliffside hotel with her mother for an hour, and already it was as crumpled and stretched as her nerves.

Her mother gave a little sniff and turned back to the bay. 'I must say you're incredibly short-tempered these days, Lucinda. I don't think all that conservation nonsense is doing you any good at all.'

Lucie gripped the railing a little more tightly than necessary and stared out across the immaculate view of the Mediterranean. The water was flat as sheet glass. The sun was halfway up in a cloudless sky. The air was light and bright. It was a beautiful day for her brother to be married, and nothing—not even her mother's fractious moods—was going to ruin it.

'We've been through this twice already, but I don't mind saying it all over again—just so we're clear.'

She turned, leaned back on the railing and waited until her mother had lowered her glass of orange juice.

'My decisions are none of your business. My job at the CCC, my choice of friends, the colour of my nail varnish—none of those or anything else is up for discussion.'

Lady Vivienne sniffed a little more and raised her glass to her lips.

'Is that quite clear, Mother?'

'You've no need to be quite so brutal about it.'

'Yes, I do. And until you stop interfering *brutal* is exactly what to expect.'

'I won't say another word,' said her mother, raising her eyebrows and tottering over on ridiculously high heels to join her.

'Let's not spoil Simon's day, hmm? God knows he's had a lot of growing up to do these past months,' said Lucie. 'Surely we can hold it together for him for one day?'

'Well, he should have thought of that before the Brigadier caught him with his daughter and we ended up footing the bill for this wedding. But I agree. You're right. As always.'

'The last thing he needs is any more worry or upset.'

Hadn't there been enough of that? she thought. Just as she'd been about to drag herself from her burrow in Petit Pierre she'd had to field another barrage of calls from her mother about this. But she'd crossed the Rubicon by then. And no amount of whining from the other side of the Atlantic would have made her budge. Her mother had to learn to step back and let Simon sort out his own mess. Which he had. Admirably!

They both turned to stare out at the bay, which was lined with criss-crosses of berthed yachts near the shore, and further out to where two huge vessels had now dropped anchor.

'Oh, I say! I'm sure I recognise that one,' said Lady Viv, lifting the binoculars to her eyes and straining forward. 'What's that flag? Blue and white. Isn't that the Argentine flag? And the name. The *Sea Devil*...'

'What? What did you say? Give me those!'

Lucie's stomach whirled. She grabbed the binoculars from her mother. Pushed them against her eyes and tried desperately to see those beloved words amongst all the sparkling white fibreglass of the yacht.

'Is that his? That polo player? Is *that* whose boat it is?'

Lucie's stomach continued to churn and her heart began to race. She scanned the yacht. There were people on it. Male, female, uniformed, casual... Walking up and down the decks, cleaning, prepping, lounging... But none of them was him. There was no sign of the tall, strong, handsome man of her heart and her dreams. Where could he be? Below? In that beautiful bedroom? Staring out at the bay? How awful if he was here with a new girlfriend. She couldn't stand it. After all she had been through, simply hearing his name was too much most days. Thinking of him with anyone else was a place she wasn't ready to travel to.

'Yes, it's the *Sea Devil*. It's Dante's yacht,' she whispered, hardly believing her eyes, hardly aware she had just said his name. 'But he's not there. I can't see him.'

'That's because he's here, Princess.'

She dropped the binoculars. She spun around. She took two paces. He stood framed in the French doors, beside the table scattered with crockery, glasses and food where they'd just breakfasted.

He was wearing a white shirt and a wary smile.

He looked at her with those eyes that startled her with their intensity in that face that winded her with its male beauty.

'Who is this, Lucie?'

Lady Viv, like a wisp of smoke, appeared at her side.

'My name is Dante Salvatore Vidal Hermida. I apologise for the interruption, but I'm here to speak to Lucie.'

His eyes never left hers.

'Did you know about this, Lucie?'

'Excuse us, Mother.'

They waited, immobile, until the clicking of heels faded and the French doors were firmly closed.

'I didn't contact you.'

She swallowed, her mind running over all the possibilities.

'I know.'

'I got lost, Lucie. I've been lost. For years.'

She gazed into his earnest face, so familiar, yet so new.

'I'm sorry. For what I did. For how I treated you. I have so much to say to you.'

She nodded. A huge swell, a tidal wave of emotion, suddenly bloomed from her heart, choking her. Her eyes burned and her throat opened on a single sob. How long had she held herself together, waiting for this moment? She clutched her arms around her body, hugging herself tightly in case part of her flew away.

'My angel. I love you. Can you forgive me?'

He walked towards her, then stopped a pace away. His face was grave, his cheeks hollow, his eyes sincere. He held his arms at his sides, palms open, as if he was offering his heart in the only way he could. And she knew she could take it or leave it. That knowledge alone unleashed her last ounce of control.

'I don't know, Dante. You hurt me more than anyone has ever hurt me. You denied me. You denied *us*.'

His eyes clenched shut at that. A shadow of pain crossed his face.

'I know. And I've lived with that since the moment you left. It will live with me for ever—unless you give me another chance.'

She looked at him—her protector, her defender, her healer. The man to whom she'd given herself— on every level. But he was damaged. He was cold. Her heart had been trampled once. Letting him back into her life was so, so risky. She couldn't have more of those times—she had barely survived this one.

She glanced away from his penetrating gaze to the railing and the bay beyond. Wedding guests were arriving—there and in the town. Preparations would already be underway here in the hotel.

'My brother is getting married today,' she said simply. 'I woke up this morning hoping that I might feel some happiness, some joy when I watched him with his bride.' She shook her head. 'Of all the people to be married—but it does seem to be the right thing…for both of them.'

'I want to marry *you*, Lucie. I want all of you— only you. No one else.'

She smiled as her throat closed over another sob. She couldn't answer. It was too huge. It was too soon.

'Did you sail here?' was all she said.

He swallowed, looked away. 'No. Flew. But the *Sea Devil* wasn't far, and I told the crew to get her here by today.'

There was a noise from inside—the muffled sound of something falling on the tiled floor—Dante glanced behind him.

'How has it been with your mother? Did you get stuff sorted?'

She nodded. 'Dante…' She clasped her hands in an entreaty. 'I waited for this moment. Months. I prayed that you would come. Or call. Or text. Anything. And you were completely silent. You knew how I felt. Yet you offered me not a single crumb of comfort.'

'I will apologise until my dying day for hurting you. But I didn't know how I felt—how to feel, even. I was so determined to get back to the life I knew—and to build the foundation with Marco—I couldn't let myself go there. I didn't know I even *could* go there. I've never felt like this—it's like a sickness, Lucie, not having you in my life.'

In the village square a clock sounded the half-hour. Lucie looked past Dante's shoulder. Shapes and shadows moved behind the glass. She should be getting ready now, her mother, but no doubt she was hovering indoors, behind a twitching curtain.

'Dante, my brother is about to get married. My mother is having kittens in there…'

'I don't give a damn about any of them. I only care about *us*!' he thundered.

'No, you only give a damn about *you*!' she thundered back. 'Did you care when I was pleading with you in New York? When I literally begged you to give us a chance? *No.* But you turn up here now, ready to lay out the cloths of heaven at my feet. Back then you wouldn't even give me the lint from your pocket.'

His eyes widened in surprise.

'Did you *really* think after what you did that you would click your fingers and I'd come running? Do you understand what you did to me?'

She stepped forward now, her anger stoked.

'You built me up. You gave me confidence to be myself—with you, and with other people. You actually made me believe in myself, and believe that I had something valuable to offer. That I was more than just Lady Vivienne's awkward daughter.'

'And you *are*,' he said quietly. 'Way more. You're a wonderful woman. You're everything to me. I'm only sorry it took me this long to say these words to you.'

'You built me up and then you threw me down. You treated me worse than my mother ever did. Because she's oblivious. But you *knew* what you were doing. And as long as you got out without anything sticking that was all that mattered.'

He closed his eyes, screwed them up, and though it hurt her to see it, she'd had to say it—had to tell him straight.

'I'll spend the rest of my life making it up to you,' he said.

And when she looked again into those eyes the blue blazed with an honesty, an integrity that she felt deep within. There was no mask. There was no façade. There was nothing but the living, breathing truth and goodness and beauty of this man.

As if a rock had rolled away from her path, as if the day had suddenly brightened with colours she had never seen, as if her whole life had fallen into place, she realised that her future was right here in this moment—ripe and ready for her to make a choice.

'And how do you propose to do that?' she said, unable to disguise the softening in her voice.

He smiled, and a tiny hint of a single dimple appeared. 'Are you leading the witness with that question?'

She smiled too, trying to hold her emotions inside as joy began a sing-song chorus from within.

'Would you object if I was?'

His smile deepened. His eyes crinkled. She saw two dimples. He stepped closer. And then he kneeled before her.

Lucie's hand flew to her chest as she gasped.

'Princess—Lucie. Love of my life. Will you marry me? Will you promise never to leave me? Will you let me love you and cherish you for ever? Because I will.'

Her head began to nod, her eyes began to stream, and the words she had never dared imagine she would say sang from her lips.

'I will. Oh, yes, I will.'

He stood, scooped her into his arms. He kissed her long and hard, and with every fibre of her being she kissed him back, loved him back.

Her eyes found his, her body melted into his, and her world righted itself on its axis.

'Your mother should be told. Before we go to this wedding.'

'She should, yes. Shall we…?'

With one final kiss he scooped her under his arm and turned them around. Their outline was one form against the beautiful clear day. And above them the hot, bright summer sun spilled light across the bay.

* * * * *

If you enjoyed this first part of Bella Frances's
CLAIMED BY A BILLIONAIRE *duet,*
look out for the second instalment

THE ITALIAN'S VENGEFUL SEDUCTION
Available May 2017!

Available April 18, 2017

#3521 THE SHEIKH'S BOUGHT WIFE
Wedlocked!
by Sharon Kendrick

Marry for money? Jane Smith would normally laugh in Sheikh Zayed's handsome face—but her sister's debts need paying. Zayed must marry to inherit his land—and plain Jane is a convenient choice. But he hasn't bargained on Jane's delicious curves...

#3522 THE MAGNATE'S TEMPESTUOUS MARRIAGE
Marrying a Tycoon
by Miranda Lee

Scott McAllister thinks Sarah is the perfect wife, until he's led to believe she committed the ultimate betrayal. Sarah's defiant response to these lies sparks Scott's desire! In a fight to save their marriage, their bed becomes the battleground...

#3523 BOUND BY THE SULTAN'S BABY
Billionaires & One-Night Heirs
by Carol Marinelli

Sultan Alim spent one forbidden night with Gabi—when he encounters her again, she refuses to name her child's father. Alim will seduce the truth out of Gabi, even if he has to lure her under false pretenses. Alim craves her, but as a mistress or bride?

#3524 DI MARCELLO'S SECRET SON
The Secret Billionaires
by Rachael Thomas

Antonio Di Marcello unexpectedly meets Sadie Parker while working undercover. Four years after their fling, he's confronted with the consequences... Sadie finds herself battling to resist Antonio's sensual onslaught—and his resolve to claim her and her son!

HPCNM0417RA

#3525 THE FORCED BRIDE OF ALAZAR
Seduced by a Sheikh
by Kate Hewitt
Azim al Bahjat stuns Alazar with his return to his kingdom and must claim his betrothed. Beguiling Johara's every instinct is to run. But as he shows her how intoxicating their wedding night could be, she begins to consider surrender...

#3526 THE INNOCENT'S SHAMEFUL SECRET
Secret Heirs of Billionaires
by Sara Craven
Alexis Constantinou haunts Selena Blake's every memory—she dreams every night of the scorching affair that stole her innocence. Seeing Alexis again, Selena cannot ignore their passion—but does she dare reveal the truth she's hidden? The secret Constantinou heir!

#3527 BLACKMAILED DOWN THE AISLE
by Louise Fuller
Billionaire Rollo Fleming catches Daisy Maddox sneaking into his office and demands she become the wife he needs for a business deal! With every kiss, Daisy's guard melts, and she discovers *pleasurable* advantages to being blackmailed down the aisle...

#3528 THE ITALIAN'S VENGEFUL SEDUCTION
Claimed by a Billionaire
by Bella Frances
Marco Borsatto gave Stacey her first taste of pleasure...only to accuse her of betrayal. She refuses to be hurt again and Marco isn't a man to forgive. But when he rescues her, it reignites an electrifying magnetism they never fully explored...

YOU CAN FIND MORE INFORMATION ON UPCOMING HARLEQUIN® TITLES, FREE EXCERPTS AND MORE AT WWW.HARLEQUIN.COM.

HPCNM0417RB

SPECIAL EXCERPT FROM

Persuading plain Jane to marry him was easy enough—
but Sheikh Zayed Al Zawba hadn't bargained on the
irresistible curves hidden under her clothes or that she
is deliciously untouched. When Jane begins to tempt
him beyond his wildest dreams, leaving their marriage
unconsummated becomes impossible…

Read on for a sneak preview of
Sharon Kendrick's book
THE SHEIKH'S BOUGHT WIFE.

Wedlocked!
Conveniently wedded, passionately bedded!

It was difficult to be distant when her body seemed to have developed a stubborn will of its own. When she found herself wanting to push her aching breasts against Zayed's powerful chest as he caught her in his arms for the traditional first dance between bride and groom. As it was, she could barely think straight and wasn't it the most infuriating thing in the world that he immediately seemed to pick up on that?

"You seem to be having trouble breathing, dear wife," he murmured as he moved her to the center of the marble dance floor.

"The dress is very tight."

"I'd noticed." He twirled her around, holding her back a little. "It looks very well on you."

She forced a tight smile but she didn't relax. "Thank you."

"Or maybe it is the excitement of having me this close to you which is making you pant like a little kitten?"

"You're annoying me, rather than exciting me. And I do wish you'd stop trying to get underneath my skin."

"Don't you like people getting underneath your skin, Jane?"

"No," she said honestly. "I don't."

"Why not?"

She met the blaze of his ebony eyes and suppressed a shiver. "Does everything have to have a reason?"

"In my experience, yes." There was a pause. "Has a man hurt you in the past?"

This was her chance to tell him yes—even though the very idea that someone had got that close to her was laughable.

Zayed had already guessed she might be a virgin, but that didn't even come close to her shameful lack of experience.

Trying to ignore the way his groin was brushing against her as he edged her closer, she glanced up at him, her cheeks burning. "I refuse to answer that on the grounds that I might incriminate myself. Tell me instead, do you always insist on interrogating women when you're dancing with them?"

"No. I don't," he said simply. "But then I've never had a bride before and I've never danced with a woman who was so determined not to give anything of herself away."

"And that's the only reason you want to know," she said quietly. "Because you like a challenge."

"All men like a challenge, Jane." His black eyes gleamed. "Haven't you learned that by now?"

She didn't answer—because how was she qualified to answer any questions about what men did or didn't like?

HARLEQUIN

Presents.

Next month, look out for *Bound by the Sultan's Baby* by Carol Marinelli—a story of a scandalous royal consequence and a billionaire determined to stake his claim!

One night with innocent wedding planner Gabi was all Sultan Alim al-Lehan allowed himself. But when duty dictates he must marry, memories of their forbidden pleasure prove impossible to forget—especially when he discovers Gabi has just returned from maternity leave!

The baby *must* be his, but if Gabi won't tell him, Alim will seduce the truth out of her! Commanding she arrange his wedding, even if he's not yet picked a wife, is the ideal ruse. Alim wants her in his bed but must decide—will she be a sultan's mistress or bride?

Don't miss

BOUND BY THE SULTAN'S BABY

Available May 2017

Get 2 Free Books,
Plus 2 Free Gifts—
just for trying the Reader Service!

Get 2 Free Books,
Plus 2 Free Gifts—
just for trying the Reader Service!